FAMILY
GUARDIAN

FAMILY GUARDIAN

•

Laurie Alice Eakes

AVALON BOOKS
NEW YORK

Published by Thomas Bouregy & Co., Inc.
160 Madison Avenue, New York, NY 10016

Library of Congress Cataloging-in-Publication Data

Eakes, Laurie Alice.
        Family guardian / Laurie Alice Eakes.
            p.   cm.
        ISBN 0-8034-9797-0 (acid-free paper)
        I. Title.

    PS3605.A377F36   2006
    813'.6—dc22

                            2006008519

PRINTED IN THE UNITED STATES OF AMERICA
ON ACID-FREE PAPER
BY HADDON CRAFTSMEN, BLOOMSBURG, PENNSYLVANIA

To my parents, who taught me to believe in the power of books, and to my husband, who taught me to believe in the power of love, I dedicate this novel.

Chapter One

Clarissant Behn dove behind the hedgerow. Kneeling in the moist earth beneath the hawthorn bushes, she peeked through the branches to see who in his right-or-wrong-mind thought a seven-o'clock-in-the-morning call acceptable behavior. Not even deliverymen arrived so early for fear of waking the family. But as clearly as blackbirds and thrushes announced a late spring morning, clopping hooves and rumbling, crunching wheels proclaimed the imminent arrival of a vehicle.

She didn't want the inconsiderate caller to see her wearing a faded gown that barely skimmed the tops of her half-boots, and her black hair in a single plait down her back. So she decided to hide behind the shrubbery until the vehicle passed, then slip around the stable to enter the house through the kitchen. Depending on the identity of the visitor and his business, she might be stuck for hours. That meant not collecting the violets in their prime. In turn, that would likely force her to pur-

1

chase the oil instead of making her own, and with all the extra expenses of her overdue come-out, she could ill afford that most costly of fragrances.

"Drat and double drat."

If only her sister, Rowena, had arrived yesterday as she planned, this wouldn't be a matter of concern. Rowena could send any interloper about his business with a lift of one golden brow.

The wheels drew nearer. No squeak accompanied the rumble of turned wood across crushed stone, so the vehicle must be well-sprung, even new. Or a farm cart that didn't have springs? No, not loud enough for a cart or wagon. It was a light vehicle.

Careful not to scratch her face on the hawthorn spines, Clarissant leaned closer to an opening in the hedge. She could just make out the right leader of what must be a four-horse team, a dark bay shining in the spring sunlight, its muscles rippling in a smooth though leisurely gait.

The visitor appeared not to be in a hurry.

Clarissant tilted her head in an effort to see the vehicle itself and perhaps the driver too. She saw a bee instead, hovering just in front of the violet she'd tucked behind her left ear.

Every muscle in her body tensed. She locked her teeth together to stop from screaming.

The bee buzzed merrily around Clarissant's head, dove into her basket of blossoms like a kingfisher after breakfast in the sea, then returned to circle her ear. She held perfectly still, trying hard not to breathe.

The caller drew nearer, close enough for her to see the entire matched team and vehicle. The latter was a high-perch phaeton, and she couldn't see the driver from behind the shrubbery unless she tilted her head back.

She dared not tilt her eyelashes upward, let alone her entire head, for fear she might startle the bee.

Oh, why didn't the vehicle move faster?

The leader drew abreast of her hiding place. The nearby birds stilled their chorus, except for the scolding crow. Clarissant caught the pungent aroma of hot horseflesh and noticed flecks of foam on his dark red sides. Though creeping along the Monmouth Park drive, the phaeton had sped sometime in the recent past. Now the driver cooled down the horses.

Or dawdled on the way to his arrival?

At the pace he drove, he would take another quarter-hour to be out of her line of sight. Meanwhile, the bee persisted, darting in and out of the flower behind her ear like one partner in a minuet. If he touched her . . .

The phaeton moved past her, a shiny black wheel rising another two feet above her head. Only dust marred the perfection of the paint. The lack of too many chips and scratches signified a new vehicle driven no more than a score or so miles. She couldn't think of a single neighbor who would purchase a sporting carriage like a phaeton. Even less could she imagine any of them so much as awaking this early, and most certainly not making calls. If this was an emergency, they'd ride horseback and not spare the horse until they reached the house.

The phaeton driver—most likely a man—must be lost. That seemed the only logical explanation. He didn't intend to call on the Behn family at all.

Relief set the pent-up breath from Clarissant's lips in

a gust that jerked her head just a little. Just enough to startle the foraging bee. With a buzz loud enough to hear above the receding wheels, the insect struck.

Clarissant screamed as white-hot pain seared through her temple. Bile burned in her throat, and for a heart-stopping moment, she feared she would faint. She clapped a hand to the root of the pain, touched the imbedded stinger, and cried out again.

A dozen yards away, the phaeton stopped.

Blinded with pain, Clarissant scrambled to her feet, and fled.

Tristan Apking jerked the reins, halting the team. "What was that?"

"Dunno," McLeod, his groom, answered. "Somebody screamin'."

"That's what I thought."

Tristan tossed the reins to the groom, then leaped the five feet to the ground and sprinted back along the drive.

Tall enough to see over the hedgerow, he caught a glimpse of someone racing between oaks and a carpet of violets. The scent robbed his breath for a moment. He blinked, nearly losing sight of the girl.

Though tall and lanky with a loose braid and short gown, she ran as though a pack of hungry hounds chased her.

Tristan slid his gaze up and down the hedgerow, seeking a way through. Nothing but dense, prickly foliage met his eyes—a wall as impenetrable as the enchanted hedge around Sleeping Beauty's castle.

The girl didn't run like anyone sleeping; she sprinted

like a yearling colt, all long-legged grace. Surely if she ran that quickly nothing could be wrong. Still . . .

He returned to the phaeton, stepped onto one of the wheels, and swung himself onto the high-perched seat.

"See anythin', sir?" McLeod asked.

"A girl running." Tristan took the reins from the groom and snapped them over the horses' backs to get them moving. "She was running, so she must be all right. I didn't see anything chasing her."

But she had screamed—twice.

He glanced toward the park. With the advantage of the phaeton's height, he caught a better look at the fleeing figure. She ran parallel to the drive about a hundred feet away, ran toward the house. He would reach it before her and could inform someone that a young woman had screamed as he passed her, then fled.

He shot a glance her way again. She'd fallen, and he caught a glimpse of her face.

"Whoa, there." He drew up the horses beside the hedgerow and stood on the footboard.

"Sir, what are you about?" McLeod cried.

The young lady stopped running and flung up her hands as though to shield her face. Despite the distance, Tristan recognized her. His heart leaped at the sight of his old friend, the child who'd shadowed him upon every visit. She wasn't whom he truly wanted to see, and the sisterly connection to his beloved Rowena made him feel closer to his lady love.

Joy welling inside him, he cupped his hands around his mouth. "Clarie!" he shouted. "Clarissant Behn!"

Her hands dropped. He saw her mouth open in surprise, a dark contrast to her pale skin. Then she lowered her head and sped in the opposite direction.

Tristan took a flying leap over the hedgerow. The slick soles of his brand new hessian boots slid on the dew-damp grass. He staggered, caught his balance, then raced in pursuit. She was fast. She always had been. Her short, muslin skirt billowed around her like sails driving a merchantman across the sea. As he chased her through a sea of flowers—violets, lavender, hyacinth and rows of lilac bushes not yet in bloom—he recalled when Bedevere Park was overgrown oaks and tangled underbrush.

But she was the Clarissant he remembered, always running, laughing, teasing. He couldn't imagine her screaming.

Tristan pushed himself to go faster and began to close the distance. She was slowing. Now she was stumbling, one hand to the side of her face, her plait falling over her shoulder.

"Clarie." He reached her side and touched the back of her hand with the tip of one finger.

She jumped and glanced up. Her dark eyes sparkled in the sunlight. Droplets shimmered on her long lashes, and a swelling pulled the corner of one eye up like a cat's. Her eyes widened, and her lips formed a perfect, pink-rimmed O, as she took a step backward. "Tristan, you're dead." Her voice was husky, hushed and a little tremulous.

Tristan's own eyes widened. "Dead? You thought I was dead?"

"Yes, we heard—" She shook her head, bewildered. "Years ago . . ."

He grinned. "A false rumor, as you can see. I'm as flesh and blood as any man, as you can see."

"But—" She blushed. Then she smiled at him with all the radiance he remembered, displaying the minute chip in her front tooth, and spread her arms as though about to fling herself against his chest.

He braced himself for the impact. The last time she'd embraced him—the day he left England—she'd knocked him off his feet.

But she stiffened and pulled herself to her full height. "Welcome to Bedevere Park."

Tristan stared at her. He didn't want her to bowl him over, but the cool formality of her greeting sent his senses reeling and his heart plummeting.

He held out both of his hands to her. "What, no embraces from my favorite hoyden?"

"I'm no longer your—a hoyden. That is to say—" She glanced down.

He followed her gaze to a faded, grass-stained skirt short enough to display fine ankles in their scuffed and muddy half-boots, and arched his brows.

She grimaced, then winced. Her hand flew to her temple where the swelling looked a bit worse.

"What happened here?" He brushed her hand aside.

She gasped. "Bee sting."

No wonder she'd screamed.

"Nasty place for it. May I help?"

"No, Mossy, Miss Moss, she'll be up and about." She turned away. "If you'll excuse me, I'll have her see to it. You go on to the house, and we'll join you shortly." She paused. "Your sister is here."

"Gwen? Here?" His heart lightened again. "Whatever—never you mind that now. Let me see if the stinger is still in there."

"It is."

"Then it should come out sooner than later."

"Another few moments won't make a difference." She started walking again.

He fell into step beside her. "Clarie, the house is in the opposite direction."

"Oh, right." Strawberry-pink spots bloomed on her cheeks, but the rest of her face was unnaturally pale, and she shook hard enough for him to see it.

He lengthened his stride and blocked her path, forcing her to stop. "Cease being a widgeon, child. You look about to faint. Let me get that stinger out." He smiled at her. "It's not like I haven't done it before."

The color over her cheeks deepened to crimson.

Tristan tightened the corners of his mouth to stop from grinning at her discomfort. She was probably too old now to want to be reminded that that bee sting had occurred on her ankle, a rather delicate place to touch for a male, even one like an older brother to her.

But then he hoped to be a true older brother to her. A brother-in-law.

With the consideration that she was likely out of the schoolroom by now, though she looked no older than sixteen, he didn't brace her chin in his hand, though it would make the job easier. "Tilt your head," was all he said.

She obeyed, squeezing her eyes shut.

He leaned close to her, catching the heady fragrance of violets for a tantalizing moment, then losing the scent in the next breath. He didn't lose the stinger. There in the middle of the swelling, marring the smooth skin of her face, it quivered.

"Ready?" he asked.

She gulped.

He plucked the stinger out.

Her breath hissed in through her teeth, and the crimson spots vanished. "Thank . . . you."

"Always at your service." He bowed. "Thank you for not screaming. Now, may I offer you a ride to the house in my phaeton?"

She turned her face away from him. "Thank you, no, I'd rather not go through the front. If Mama is awake and sees me like this, she'll have strong hysterics."

"Heaven forfend. Might she not have them anyway, seeing me again?"

"Depending on whether or not she's had her morning chocolate. If she hasn't yet drunk it, she may think you a ghost."

Tristan's heart lightened even further. "Comfort in knowing Lady Monmouth hasn't changed. And your father?"

"I'm sorry, Tristan. He passed away eighteen months ago."

"Ah, Clarie, I am sorry." For himself, considering how the Viscount Monmouth had treated him, his sorrow didn't run deep, but for Clarissant's sake, sadness touched his heart. "You always were his favorite."

"I do miss him dearly." She touched her temple. "We'll talk more over breakfast. Gwen will be overjoyed, and you'll be amazed to see what a young gentleman my brother Dunstan has become." She spun on her heel and trotted toward a gap in the hedge.

"Clarie, wait." Tristan strode after her. "What about Rowena?"

"She isn't here."

A shiver ran up his spine. "Clarie, she isn't . . . she hasn't . . . like your father?"

Her smile held sympathy and sorrow. "No, Rowena is well. You'll see her soon enough." As she slipped through the gap in the hedge, he thought he heard her mutter, "Too soon."

Clarie flew down the kitchen passageway, startling a maid into dropping a plate of toast, and took the back-stairs two at a time. The instant her foot reached the landing, she started to call out. "Gwenevere, Mossy, where are you? You won't believe who is arriving. Oh, where are—"

Doors banged open along the corridor. Miss Moss, former governess and now general companion, popped her head around the edge of her bedchamber door, nightcap still in place. Gwen stood in her doorway, dressing gown clutched around her, the sash trailing, and her hair tumbling in deep red curls down her back.

"Where do you expect us to be?" Miss Moss demanded in a scratchy voice. "It's barely past seven o'-clock."

Gwen's gray-green eyes sparkled. "Who? Not my brother."

For a moment, Clarissant felt deflated, thinking Gwen already knew. Then she realized that her friend meant her elder brother, and she laughed. "Yes, but not Percival."

"What?" Gwen's mouth dropped open, then she snapped it shut. "Clarissant Behn, that isn't in the least an amusing jest."

"Especially not at this hour," Miss Moss added. "You are far too old for your pranks, Miss Clarissant."

"I'm not jesting." Clarissant glanced from one lady to the other. "It's true. I saw him. I spoke to him." He'd touched her hand with one finger and expected one of her childish, exuberant hugs. "It's truly Tristan. He's not in the least dead."

Gwen still looked dubious.

Miss Moss looked annoyed. "Miss Clarissant—"

Hammering on the knocker resounded up the main staircase.

Clarissant gestured to the front of the house. "You can see for yourself. It's Tristan as I live and breathe— living and breathing himself and looking prosperous."

Looking fine with his deep red hair cut to wave beneath his top hat, and wearing a coat of blue superfine and fawn-colored pantaloons that fit him to perfection. New clothes. Well-tailored clothes. And a carriage and team that cost a fortune.

He'd set off to make one.

Gwen stood like a garden statue, wide-eyed and pale.

Miss Moss' frown deepened. "How badly did I teach you, for you to speak to gentlemen dressed like that and with—whatever happened to your face?"

"Bee sting."

Downstairs, a footman opened the front door. Voices drifted from the marble entry hall.

"I can wait if no one is about yet," Tristan said.

Gwen jumped, clasped a hand across her mouth, then flung herself into Clarissant's arms. "You weren't funning. Oh, Clarie, it's true. It's true. It's true." Though four inches shorter than Clarissant and far more delicately boned, she managed to spin her around in a circle.

Laughing, Clarissant hugged her friend and joined in the impromptu dance. "I wouldn't fun about that. It's true. He's alive."

"Then I suggest you get dressed so you may go see him," Miss Moss said.

"Yes, of course." Gwen released Clarissant fast enough to send her reeling against the wall and dashed into her bedchamber. "Won't he be pleased to see me so grown up?" The wardrobe door creaked open. "And just in time for my come-out. He'll make it bearable." A gown flew across the doorway to land somewhere near the bed. "This is a miracle, a joy, a—"

The abrupt cessation of speech and activity startled Clarissant out of her pleasure in her friend's excitement and back to the reality of the difficulties that were inevitable with Tristan's return. Gwen must have drawn the same conclusions as Clarissant, for she appeared in the doorway, a petticoat draped over one arm and a pair of stockings over the other.

"Clarissant," she demanded in dramatic accents, "please tell me he didn't ask about Rowena."

Clarissant sighed. "He did in such a way . . ." She glanced at Miss Moss, who also looked concerned.

"Then he's still enamored of her?" Gwen asked.

"I believe so," Clarissant answered around a heavy

heart. "The way he looked, when he asked about her, it seems more than likely."

"Poor lad," Miss Moss murmured.

"Poor us," Gwen said. "We have to decide which one of us is going to tell him that Rowena is married."

Chapter Two

Her face throbbing, Clarissant followed Gwen downstairs to where Miss Moss said she would entertain Tristan in the breakfast room. She didn't need as much time as Clarissant and Gwen to ready herself, for Gwen wished her brother to see her looking like a fashionable young lady of nineteen, not a ragamuffin miss from the schoolroom. Clarissant didn't want to see him at all, not if she must be the one to inform him that Rowena had not, as she promised, waited for him forever.

She hadn't waited for two months. But Clarissant would protect Tristan from that information at all cost.

Besides, Clarissant's face looked as bad as it felt, according to her mirror and Gwen's cheerful bluntness. The swelling over her temple, a lurid purple in color, pulled the corner of her eye up in a decidedly feline manner. Compared with her other only mildly almond-shaped eye, the effect gave her a lopsided aspect that made her top knot of curls appear as though they were about to slip sideways, or that she wore one high-heeled and one heelless slipper.

But Tristan was alive. Despite the realization that he still thought of her as a mere whelp, and despite the fact that he had come to see Rowena—who no longer lived at Bedevere Park, and hadn't for five and a half years—Clarissant's heart felt lighter than it had since her mother insisted she should have a come-out season.

Ahead of Clarissant, Gwen danced down the stairs, the ribbons holding up her dark-red ringlets bouncing like plumage on a parade horse. Her Pomona-green gown puffed and billowed around her, suggesting that she lifted her knees as though dancing a jig. Though her heart felt as if it raced ahead of her with the same prancing steps Gwen employed, Clarissant made her feet move with dignity one step at a time. Her own lavender muslin gown flowed around her legs, and she barely showed the toes of her ivory kid slippers. She held her head steady and high.

A little too high. With her gaze fixed on the fan-shaped window above the front door, she didn't notice that Tristan had come into the entry hall until Gwen shrieked and leaped the last three steps to fling herself into her brother's arms.

Clarissant's hands dropped to her sides. She bunched her skirt and petticoat into her fists, preparing to lift them to make the jump. How she longed to join the embracing and laughing and, from Gwen, tears of joy in the marble chamber. Three years ago, she would have. Out of sight of any servants, she would cavort in glee. But not in front of the servants. Not in front of Tristan.

Because he still treated her like a child.

But she was grown enough to know love—and a broken heart.

I was nearly a woman grown, when you left.

Clarissant released her gown and paced down the last three steps. She then stood motionless, one hand on the newel post, waiting for Gwen to cease mauling her brother.

He extricated himself. Laughing, he strode across the floor to hold out his hand to Clarissant. "Is this the same lady I saw in the park earlier?"

"Did you see someone in the park earlier?" Clarissant returned.

"That must have been the scullery maid," Gwen said.

Clarissant smiled, blessing her friend.

"Hmm." Tristan touched one finger to the swelling beside Clarissant's left eye. "A maid and lady stung in the same place. A sorry morning for the bees."

"No, no," Gwen said, "she fell out of bed."

"Indeed." Tristan grinned at his sister, then gave Clarissant a sober look. "Does your face hurt you overly much?"

"Only when I look in the mirror." The quip popped out before she could stop herself.

Tristan narrowed his eyes. "You haven't changed, have you?"

Clarissant wanted to say, "My hems are down, and my hair is up, in the event you haven't noticed," but chose a silent smile instead. If he couldn't notice the changes for himself, she wasn't one to tell him.

"She's six years older," Gwen said. She danced toward the breakfast room. "Shall we eat? I'm famished."

"Miss Gwenevere," Mossy's voice rumbled from the doorway, "a lady never admits to appetite."

"To a gentleman," Gwen pointed out. "But this is my brother."

"And speaking of brothers . . ." Clarissant turned to the sound of heels clattering down a side passage.

Already as tall as her shoulder at the age of twelve, Dunstan, Lord Monmouth, raced into the entry hall, his blond hair wind-blown, his hands and face smudged with something that looked like black garden dirt, and his pockets bulging and—heaven forefend—squirming. "Clarie, you should see the bang-up phaeton outside. Do we have—" He skidded to a halt and performed an elegant bow. "Forgive me, sir, I didn't notice you there." He cast Clarissant a questioning glance.

"You likely don't remember Tristan Apking, do you?" she said.

"Apking?" Dunstan's Wedgwood-blue eyes widened. "But you're dead."

Tristan returned the bow. "A grossly exaggerated rumor, my lord."

"Well, apparently, but—" Dunstan's face paled beneath the grime, and he clamped a hand to a now flat pocket.

"Did you lose something?" Clarissant asked, already scanning the floor.

"Just a wee little snake."

"Snake?" Gwen and Mossy chorused.

They fled. The breakfast room door slammed.

Clarissant felt a light, wriggling weight on her right toe and lifted her hem. A green snake not much larger than a pencil crept across her slipper. "If one of you gentlemen will be so kind and remove this poor creature to the garden?"

Dunstan snatched it up. "Sorry. I'll, um, just take it up . . ." Head bowed, he headed for the stairs, pocket bulging again.

Tristan clamped a hand on his shoulder and spun him toward the door. "You'll take that poor creature to the garden as your sister told you to do, and leave it there."

"But—"

"Go," Clarissant said.

Feet dragging, Dunstan retreated down the passageway.

"And wash before you join us for breakfast." She smiled at Tristan. "Thank you. He'd have an entire menagerie up in the schoolroom if I let him, and then Miss Moss would resign."

"Isn't he old enough for school?" Tristan asked.

"Why pay for school, when we've a perfectly good governess in Miss Moss and the vicar for advanced mathematics?"

"But a lad—" He stopped, lowered his eyes. "Schools are expensive, are they not?"

"Yes, but that's not the difficulty now. Dunstan . . . well, let's go in and assure the others the danger has passed."

Tristan turned to the breakfast parlor and held out his arm. "You didn't think it was any danger."

She couldn't see his face, and she heard the approval in his tone. Her heart skipped like Gwen.

Foolish heart.

She rested two fingers in the crook of his elbow, noting the smoothness of his wool coat and the toughness of the muscle beneath. "I'm in the gardens so much, I'd never survive if I were afraid of a little snake."

"Surely you don't do your own gardening." Tristan opened the door to the curtained-off section of the great dining room they used for breakfast. Aromas of coffee, brewing tea, and spicy sausages wafted around them. "Not with all the foliage I saw."

"No, I have several helpers." She knew she was treading on dangerous ground, talking about the extent of the flowers grown at Bedevere Park—more flowers than food—so she cast her attention to the two ladies perched on chairs, their feet drawn up beneath them.

"It's gone," she told them of the snake.

"I'll assign him extra reading today," Miss Moss declared, lowering her feet to the rug.

Clarissant seated herself in the chair Tristan drew out for her. "Not extra reading. You know that makes him worse behaved. I'll ask the vicar to give him lessons on gentlemanly behavior."

Mossy sighed. "A sad thing he doesn't have a father. A lad needs a man in the family."

"One of his sisters should marry and provide him with an elder brother," Tristan suggested.

Clarissant dug her fingernails into the sides of her chair cushion.

"Coffee or tea, Tris?" Gwen asked too quickly.

"Coffee." He sauntered to the sideboard, where silver chafing dishes held sausage, bacon and eggs. "May I fetch you some breakfast, Clarie?"

"Miss B—er, Clarissant," Mossy said.

"My apologies." Tristan bowed in Clarissant's direction. "But you'll always be little Clarie to me."

Clarissant winced. "Hardly little, unless you've been amongst the Amazons."

"*Where* have you been?" Gwen demanded.

Tristan forked sausages onto a plate. "All around the world, my dear. India, China, America—"

"America," all the ladies exclaimed.

"But we were at war with them," Gwen said.

"Not for two and a half years." Tristan piled fingers of toast onto the plate, then faced the table. "Will this do, Clarie?"

"Quite well, thank you." She drew her brows together. "If you've been flitting about the world, why did you never write to tell us you were alive?"

"I didn't know you thought I was dead." Tristan set the plate before her and returned to the sideboard. "So I wrote when I could, but that matter of a war seems to have kept my letters from reaching you." His own plate filled, he seated himself at the small, gateleg table. "Did you not receive a one?"

Clarissant and Gwen shook their heads.

"And we couldn't write to you," Gwen said. "But I kept a journal, so I can tell you all about Percival getting married and being an aunt and Clarie's venture—"

Clarissant kicked her under the table.

Gwen gasped, grabbed for the teapot, and refilled her cup. "I forgot you don't know about our nephew."

"No." Sadness crossed Tristan's face. "How old?"

"Two and a half and every bit as mischievous as Dunstan. They're expecting another interesting event in the summer. That's why they're not going to London with us."

Tristan set his knife and fork across his plate. "When do you leave for London?"

"The end of the week," Gwen said.

"If Miss Clarissant's face heals up by then," Miss Moss added.

"Oh, it must," Gwen wailed. "Rowena will have a—" she clapped her hand over her mouth too late.

Silence fell over the chamber. Outside in the entryway, light, running footfalls announced the imminent arrival of Dunstan, as a servant would never run. Inside the breakfast parlor, Gwen looked pale and Mossy grim. Clarissant felt the sausages curdle into a lump in her stomach.

Tristan took a long, deep breath, then smiled. "So where is Rowena, and when do I get to see her?"

Gwen looked at her plate, a wreck of toast crumbs and bacon rinds. "Possibly tomorrow."

"That's wonderful." Tristan resumed eating. "Did she go up to London to make advanced preparations?"

"She's been there since Easter," Clarissant said.

She dropped her hands to her lap so he couldn't see her fingers twisting together. She looked at her plate, too, so she didn't have to see his face.

His flatware clinked against the earthenware plate. "So who's chaperoning her?"

"She doesn't need a chaperone. She's . . . oh, I can't bear it!" Gwen leaped to her feet and fled, coming close to knocking down Dunstan in the doorway.

He glanced after her, then back to the room, his

face now only mildly grimy. "What's got her in a lather?"

"Something about Rowena not needing a chaperone," Tristan said, sounding as perplexed as Dunstan looked.

Dunstan wrinkled his nose. "Of course she don't need a chaperone. It ain't nothing to get distressed about. Ain't never heard of a married lady that does need one."

Tristan's feet carried him unerringly to the one oak tree in the park that remained as he remembered it. The tallest tree in the two square miles of parkland, it spread its branches studded with budding leaves over the rustic bench that surrounded the yard-thick trunk. His head resting on the rough bark, he gazed through the criss-crossed canopy to a sky so blue it made his throat ache.

His heart ached for other reasons.

Rowena was married. He knew he shouldn't have expected a lady as beautiful and sweet-natured as she was to go without a host of suitors, but she'd promised to wait for him. The fact that she had no dowry or even the funds from her family for a London season made that all the more likely. Obviously the Behns had found a source of income after all.

His eyes watering from staring into the bright morning light, he lowered his head, and saw Clarissant strolling across the grass like Demeter herself. A lavender-and-white-striped spencer hugged her arms and the bodice of her lavender muslin gown. The collar stood up in back to form a frame for her neck and face.

What a neck and face!

Tristan straightened, blinking. He'd always thought Clarie a pretty child, though nothing that would ever hold a candle to her elder sister, but she'd grown up somewhat better than commonplace pretty. Even without the distorting swelling on her right temple, her eyes formed a definite almond shape, large eyes so bright they looked blue, though he knew they were nearly black. The tight jacket and flowing skirt of the gown showed she'd left childhood behind.

She smiled at him from across the intervening gap of flower-stretched lawn.

He managed a smile back.

"What happened to the rest of the oaks?"

She paused and glanced around her. "We sold them to pay taxes and . . . debts." She continued beneath the canopy of the oak. "I wouldn't let them take them all."

"I'm glad you didn't." Tristan looked at a branch as thick as his arm protruding from the trunk ten feet above his head. "Isn't this the tree you fell out of?"

"How ungentlemanly of you to remember that." Grinning, she seated herself on the bench far enough away that he could see only the side of her face not swollen from the bee sting. "I'm truly sorry you had to learn the news like that. We didn't think to warn Dunstan."

"You were laughing all the way to the ground," Tristan said. "Then you hit the ground and lay there so still and silent I thought you were dead."

"We thought you were dead."

"But you were just stunned."

"She was already twenty. How long could you expect her to wait?"

"You waited there like a rock, while I ran for help, never complaining, even with that broken arm."

Clarissant grabbed his wrist. "I'll twist your arm if you won't listen to me."

He looked down at her hand, slim and long-fingered in white kid gloves. "I've listened to all I need to know. Rowena didn't wait for me."

"Because she thought you were dead," Clarissant cried. "How many times do I have to tell you that?"

Tristan's jaw hardened. "Repeating it doesn't make it true."

"Obviously it's not, but when we never received any letters, what were we to believe?"

"Why did you believe in my death?"

"We heard you sailed on the merchantman *Eastern Knight,* and that the French captured it in the Bay of Biscay."

Tristan stared at her, but she didn't look at him, one thing about her that had changed. Clarissant was always direct.

He narrowed his eyes. "Being captured does not mean the same thing as being dead."

"No, but—" She surged to her feet and began to pace in front of him, her hands clasped at her waist. Her head bent, she seemed intent on moving without stepping on tiny white wildflowers in the grass.

His lips in a grim line, he watched her, willing his hurt to turn into the anger of betrayal.

Clarissant stopped walking and faced him, her countenance as tight as his felt. "Tristan, the war's been over for two years. Three, if you consider that it was over the

first time in fourteen, and most of the prisoners returned. In all that time, not one word from you."

"I told you I wrote."

"But we received nothing. That adds up to you being
dead." She sighed and bowed her head again. "And we
were so poor. Rowena didn't have the come-out she deserved, and I was about to be old enough. Papa . . . you
know I loved my father, and he was . . ." She waved her
hand in the air and recommenced her pacing.

Tristan gave her a sad smile. He knew what she
meant. His own father hadn't been much different,
though their estate on the Welsh border provided them
with a fine string of horses that bred and sold under the
supervision of a responsible manager. That left Mr. Apking free to pursue his studies of Arthurian legend.
They were legends he and Lord Monmouth foisted
upon their children with their names, all six of them
cursed with monikers straight out of the annals of
Arthurian lore.

Lord Monmouth, forever insistent that he was a de-
scendant of the Monmouth who wrote a history of that
great, British king, only had land that needed careful
tending and management. Lord Monmouth was too
much of a scholar to concern himself with a man of
business who stole from him on a regular basis until the
estate hovered on bankruptcy.

"If I may be so bold," Tristan said, "you don't look
poor now."

Clarissant stumbled, stopped, stiffened. "Rowena is
sponsoring our come-out."

Some of the pain around Tristan's heart eased as he

understood her unspoken message. Rowena had married to save the family fortune, to give her younger siblings a chance in life.

"How like that sweet angel," he murmured. "She sacrificed her desires for her family."

Clarissant neither spoke nor looked at him. She stooped, began picking the tiny, white flowers and brushing them across her upper lip. Her nostrils flared, and she nodded, then tucked the blossoms into the neckline of her spencer.

"Is he a man worthy of her?" Tristan asked.

"Tom Hornwick?" Smiling, Clarissant glanced up from the wildflowers. "He's really Lord Seasham, but doesn't in the least act like one would expect an earl to. He's the dearest brother-in-law I could—" Her face reddened. "That is, the best I could have hoped for next to you."

"Titled and wealthy." Tristan stared at the boots that cost more than he'd had in his pocket, when he left England in 1811. "I couldn't give her either."

Clarissant nudged one of his boots with the toe of her kid slipper. "You're telling me you didn't make your fortune as you promised you would?"

"Well, that." Tristan shrugged. "It's of no importance now. I was going to buy a fine estate and a house in London. All those things I know Rowena wanted. I can afford that much. And more. But now . . ." He gazed across the parkland to where Rowena and he used to meet beneath another oak.

A fountain stood in its place, spraying a delicate mist from a marble water lily and watering the ferns around the base. Rowena detested fountains. She'd liked the oak with its hollow, where they could exchange secret messages, when her father forbade them to meet.

"It was dead," Clarissant said.

Tristan started and glanced at her.

"The oak," Clarissant said. "It wasn't producing any leaves, so I . . . we had to cut it down."

"That's wise." Tristan stood. "I'll say good-bye to Gwen, then ride west to see Percival and his family before I leave."

"Leave?" Clarissant grasped his arm. "Where will you go?"

"Back to sea. To America, perhaps."

"But—" She released his arm and clasped her hands over the wildflowers. "Why would you do that? We want you here."

Tristan faced her, smiled at her with all the warmth he felt for this young lady, who was as much a sister to him as Gwen. "I know you do, and I'll miss you all terribly again. But I've had my heart so set on one lady for a wife for so long, I have to plan my future again without her."

Her lower lip quivered. "You'll find someone else to love."

"Perhaps. I'd like to think so. But not here. Not in England. I need a completely new start."

Chapter Three

For the first time since she'd fallen in love with Tristan Apking when she was sixteen, Clarissant believed God had granted her the opportunity to win his heart from Rowena's, and now he planned to leave. If he did, he would not come back. His adoration of Rowena, who didn't deserve a minute of it, drew him back to England. Now it must not—absolutely must not!—drive him away for a second time. At least, it must not until Clarissant received enough time to convince him he could love her.

And how will you do that?

The question shoved a sigh from her lungs.

Beside her on the rustic bench, Tristan touched her arm. "What's amiss, Clarie?"

You calling me by that childish name.

She smiled at him, noting how the sunlight filtering through the branches sparked fire from his deep red hair. Simply looking at him sparked fire within her veins. Six years hadn't dulled her feelings in the least. Nor the pain of knowing how he adored another.

Tears blurred her eyes, and she looked away. "Will you not at least remain for your sister's coming out ball? It's only a fortnight away."

"I don't want to see Rowena." He let out a bark of mirthless laughter and tilted his head back. "I've battled pirates on the high seas and bandits in the hinterland, and I'm afraid to come face to face with one small female. What a coward you must think I am!"

"Only a bit of one." Clarissant smiled so he would know she teased him. "Of course, I only have your word about the pirates and bandits, but I can see for myself that you run from my sister."

He touched his neck, where a starched, white stock encircled his throat. "I have the scars to prove the former. They're long since healed, so the pain is gone."

"But the wound on your heart is still raw?" Clarissant tried not to grimace. "You sound more like one of the poets than a man of adventure."

He laughed. "So I do." He rose and held one hand out to her. His lips smiled, though his gray eyes held a bleakness that made Clarissant long to pull her sister's golden tresses like a six-year-old. "And you don't care to hear about either."

"On the contrary." She took his hand and rose. "I'd love to hear about the pirates and bandits."

"I'd rather forget both." He turned toward the house, a solid mass of gray stone and sparkling windows across an expanse of greensward and flowers. "But if it'll please all of you, I'll remain for the come-out ball. That'll give me time to find another ship heading to the East."

Clarissant thanked the Lord he wasn't looking at her as she took his arm. She didn't want to give away her own hurt at the idea of him running off so soon.

Running off at all.

She dug her toe into the grass. "Where in the East?"

Tristan headed for the house, covering the distance with a long, rolling stride. "New South Wales, I think."

Clarissant lengthened her own steps to keep up with him. "But that's all convicts."

"And a military that needs supplies." Tristan paused by the fountain. "Surely Rowena didn't give you a fountain. She never liked them."

"No, she doesn't. But I do." Clarissant hated to admit the origin of the fountain, for it would confirm the lie of omission she intended to practice on Tristan for the sake of his heart. "My brother-in-law gave it to me for my birthday. My twenty-first."

"Your twenty-first? Are you truly that old?"

She pinched his arm, but only managed a slight pressure on a forearm with muscle like iron beneath the soft sleeve of his coat. Shipboard life served a man's physique well, if Tristan was an example.

"I'm three and twenty now."

Tristan gave her a look of mock horror. "You can't be only four years younger than I."

Clarissant elevated her nose. "Just because I was the one bringing in the snakes before you left, doesn't mean I was twelve like Dunstan."

"I believe you only did it to make Rowena's life miserable." Tristan resumed walking, his head turned slightly away from her, as though he studied the nearby grove of lilac bushes not yet in bloom. "If you hadn't placed one in her reticule . . ." He shrugged and increased his pace, his feet crushing the warm grass and sending its spring sweetness into the air.

Clarissant walked with delicacy, a trick she'd learned, when she grew nearly as tall as her father and taller than most grown males she knew. Just because she possessed Junoesque proportions didn't mean she had to tramp around like a man.

Moving lightly through the grass enabled her to catch the snake she placed in Rowena's reticule the night she and Tristan intended to elope. As Clarissant planned, Rowena reached into her bag to make certain she carried everything she needed for a sprint to the border, encountered the snake, and screamed loudly enough to alarm Tristan waiting around a curve in the drive. Rowena only needed to scream loudly enough to awaken her parents to suit Clarissant's purpose. That Tristan began pounding on the door gave away the whole scheme. Lord Monmouth sent Tristan packing and Rowena to her aunt's house in Northumberland. Tristan went to sea. Rowena met Lord Seasham.

A twinge of guilt plucked at Clarissant for the second time since the incident—the first being more than a twinge, when she learned of Tristan's death. She attempted a bit of comfort. "Rowena would never have been happy poor."

"She said she'd be happy poor with me." Tristan's voice held no emotion.

If you believe that, you're a fool.

She wouldn't be that rude to him. Love did close a

body's mind off to the beloved's faults. She knew that. Tristan's love for Rowena showed his weakness for a pretty face rather than an accomplished mind. Men did tend to behave that way. That was one of the reasons why she'd been glad poverty, then her father's death, held her back from the performance of a coming-out season. She didn't want to discuss the weather when she needed to think about increasing her income.

She wondered where Tristan had gotten his fortune and how. Propriety wouldn't allow even an old friend to ask. Not a female asking a male.

She stumbled on the perfectly smooth lawn and halted, aghast. Propriety might stop her from asking about his apparent wealth, but what if he started asking questions about hers? She wanted him to think that Rowena married to save the family fortunes. Society believed the Behns prospered because of a generous brother-in-law. Although Tom was the best of fellows and had helped some, the truth behind the Behns' comfortable circumstances would ruin Clarissant's reputation, and would more than likely hurt Tristan so much he'd flee England immediately. If Tristan didn't learn the truth, however, he would leave England believing Rowena sacrificed her own happiness to help her family.

Aware that Tristan stared at her, Clarissant gave him a small smile. "Sorry. I was just thinking . . . would you prefer to see Rowena before or after she learns of your return?"

"Ah, that." He shrugged in a way she'd seen French émigrés do. "I'd rather she were warned first. The shock of seeing me might have adverse effect on her delicate constitution."

Clarissant wrinkled her nose. She couldn't help herself. She managed not to snort with the derision she felt.

The only matter about Tristan's return that would have an adverse effect on Rowena was seeing how fine he looked and how prosperous. Seasham matched any man for looks and surpassed most in wealth, but Tristan's looks would cast Seasham's into the shade.

And his wealth?

She resumed walking, biting her tongue to hold back the question she so wanted to ask. The distant laughter of laundry maids ringing across the garden reminded Clarissant to speak to them about not washing her smocks with the rest of the clothes. The scent of flower oils permeated everything, and Dunstan didn't like his shirts reeking of roses and violets.

She removed her hand from Tristan's arm. "If you will excuse me, I've some household matters to see to. Gwen will want to talk to you and hear all about your adventures."

He glanced at the house, where his phaeton still stood in the drive, though a groom had led the horses away. "Not a great deal to tell."

She stared at him. "You told me you fought off pirates and bandits, and now you tell me there's not much to tell? Tristan, that's unkind. You know how Gwen and I both love a good story."

He grinned. "I remember, but this one isn't precisely good."

"The story isn't, or you weren't?"

He laughed and chucked her under the chin. "Incorrigible as ever, aren't you?"

Incorrigible enough to want to punch you under the chin for treating me like a schoolgirl.

She narrowed her eyes at him. "If Gwen doesn't get it out of you, I certainly will."

"I've no doubt of that." He bowed. "I concede. When you return to the house, I'll regale you with enough tales to curl your hair—if I can hold my sister off that long."

She curtsied. "Thank you kindly, sir." Heart aching, she turned on her heel and headed across the rose garden to the door in a brick wall that sheltered the herb and kitchen garden from the flowers. Despite wanting to look behind her and watch Tristan walk away, she refrained. He mustn't catch her watching him.

As she reached the door, she asked herself why not. If she couldn't admit the truth to him about how the Behns regained their fortune for fear of hurting him, then he wouldn't discover the truth about Rowena's treacherous vow to wait for him. He would continue to believe she was an angel, a sacrificial lamb for her family's sake. He would leave still carrying a torch for a lady who didn't deserve his regard, and Clarissant would lose again unless she could change his mind and his heart.

In two weeks? She didn't see how she could manage that feat without informing him that Rowena waited for him as long as it took to find a better prospect. Yet if she did so, might he not despise the messenger? Worse, he might disbelieve her and dislike her for it. At least now they resumed their old camaraderie. That gave

Clarissant comfort along with the joy of knowing he lived. But win his heart in two weeks?

She yanked open the kitchen garden door. Newly sprouting thyme, rosemary and sage greeted her nostrils, mingling with the richness of turned earth awaiting the planting of more vegetables at the new moon, the only time her gardeners would plant anything. She planted whenever the weather suited the plant in question, and the phase of the moon didn't matter; everything she planted flourished, including the first bottled scent she sent to a local shop. That one of the Almack's patronesses found herself stranded in the village with a broken carriage wheel, wandered into the shop, found the scent and loved it helped matters immensely. She made it the fashion in London, and, at seventeen, Clarissant Behn became a secret success.

The source of the family income remained secret even to her mother, brother and friends. Like the rest of the *haut ton,* they believed that Seasham supported them. Tom, the dear fellow, wouldn't give away her secret, and Rowena didn't dare. But a husband would complicate matters. Husbands gained control of their wives' fortunes upon marriage, and few men in society would appreciate a wife who engaged in trade. Even cloaked in perfume, her business still carried the "stink of the shop."

That shop was actually a factory located in London with a manager who acted as the liaison between Clarissant—the creator of the scents—and the workers and shops that bought the products. At home in Surrey, people believed that Clarissant enjoyed an unusual and

fragrant hobby. They believed her factory manager performed the duties of a man of business such as any estate employed.

The Behns didn't employ such a man. Clarissant did
the work of overseeing the home farm and tenant farm-
ers herself. She didn't have time for balls, and drives in
the park filled with banal conversation. But Gwen
wouldn't go without her, and Gwen deserved a season.

With a dozen tasks to perform that day, Clarissant
didn't have time to linger about in the herb garden
wool-gathering. If she didn't speak to the laundresses
soon, they would wash her smocks with Dunstan's
shirts, and Gwen would hear all of Tristan's tales, for
as his sister she could ask him questions Clarissant
could not.

Clarissant hastened along the gravel path to the laundry. As she feared, the maids were about to dunk her
smocks into the water with Dunstan's shirts. They
stopped, white linen garments bundled in their arms,
and still managed to curtsy.

"I forgot to tell you." She spoke too quickly with too
little dignity, and made herself slow. "Lord Monmouth
doesn't like his shirts smelling of my scents, so will
you be so kind as to wash his shirts first?"

"Yes, miss, of course we can." Molly, the oldest
laundress at twenty-five, spoke as she set the smocks
aside. "But we were just saying it's a pity soap for the
laundry can't be so fine as that you use for washing."

Blushing, Liza, the youngest at sixteen, stepped forward. "I still use that soap you gave me for Christmas
every Sunday before church. Now Jack Marsden the
blacksmith's apprentice sits beside me every week."

Clarissant smiled. "I'm certain it's not just the soap, but when a lady smells pretty, she feels pretty, and that helps her act pretty. But what could we make the laundry soap smell like without making the gentlemen unhappy?"

"Lavender."

"Too sweet. Wildflowers?"

"Honey?"

Clarissant threw up her hands at the barrage of suggestions. "One at a time. Liza?"

Liza ducked her head, sending damp, chestnut curls tumbling over her flushed face. "Something like springtime. Like the air smells after the rain. New grass or clover."

Clarissant stared at her along with the others. "I'll think about that, Liza."

She'd think about more. She'd consider taking Liza on as an apprentice.

"Anyone else?" she asked.

They all shook their heads.

"Liza's right good at smells," Molly said.

Clarissant studied the petite maid for a moment, then nodded. "Liza, when you're finished helping with the washing, I want you to fetch a basket and pick the freshest clover you can find, then bring it to my workshop. I'll send the scullery maid out to help the rest of you hang things."

"Yes, miss." Liza curtsied, and the others followed suit.

Clarissant turned to the house and set her footfalls for the kitchen door. Behind her, the laundry remained silent. When she reached the kitchen door, a cacophony of excited chatter broke out amongst the laundresses.

She hoped her actions wouldn't alienate Liza from the other maids. It happened when one servant became elevated above the rest in rank. Yet how could she waste talent? If indeed Liza possessed talent with scents.

Her own ability would end up wasted if she married a man who didn't approve of his wife's business. Tristan would understand. He hadn't teased her as his brother and Rowena had, when Clarissant was a child crushing flowers to make herself smell pretty. Since he'd been at sea, he had presumably made his money by trade, too, not through land and rents as did true gentlemen.

Was that why he seemed reluctant to talk about it? He might fear they would look down on him.

No, he feared only Rowena looking down on him. With that in mind, Clarissant wondered why she thought she could win his heart in a lifetime, let alone two weeks, unless she somehow persuaded him to remain after the ball. Or perhaps she could pray that no ship became available right away.

Clarissant located the scullery maid and directed her to help the laundresses hang clothes. "I'll make it right with Cookie."

All she needed to do to keep the cook happy was remind her of the days she would have to sit with her feet up and sipping tea, while the family resided in London at Lady Seasham's house. That task complete, she snatched a Shrewsbury biscuit off the cooling rack and, munching, pushed through the baize-covered door leading into the entrance hall. Hearing no voices emanating from either the parlor or the library, she asked the footman by the door where Miss and Mr. Apking had gone.

"Mr. Apking has gone to the stable," the man said, "and I am sorry to say that I do not know the whereabouts of Miss Apking."

Clarissant stared at him. "They're not together?"

A head shorter than she, the footman looked past her left shoulder. "Miss Apking left the house before Mr. Apking returned, and the groom came to say that one of Mr. Apking's horses has a swelling on a hock, so he left for the stable."

Where could Gwen have gone? Surely she wanted to talk to her brother. When he excused himself from the breakfast table after learning of Rowena's marriage, Gwen burst into floods of tears. So Clarissant chose to follow him, thinking he didn't need a watering pot for comfort.

Shaking her head in bewilderment, Clarissant crossed the foyer to the front door. The footman pulled it open for her, and she exited into sparkling sunlight and the scent of the sap running in the firs lining one side of the drive.

Would that make a good scent for cleaning soap?

Nostrils flaring, mind spinning with recipes, Clarissant descended the three fan-shaped steps leading from the front door and onto the carriage sweep before the house. She could not think where to find Gwen, since she hadn't been in the park. With most of the trees gone, it no longer offered a haven for those seeking solitude.

One day, Clarissant wanted to build a summerhouse

where one could sit beneath a shady roof, yet enjoy cool, fragrant breezes while reading, sewing or simply thinking. That plan went by the wayside to pay for new gowns and other fripperies for her mother and her. Dunstan probably did not like it and this was, in truth, his property. If Clarissant didn't wed, she would need to find her own establishment. Already, she saved money for that. Her mother thought it was her dowry. It would be if she married Tristan.

She shook her head. Never should she rekindle the ashes of her dreams that one day she would marry Tristan Apking. That was the sensible notion. Her heart insisted on foolishness since she came face to face with him in the park.

Her foolish heart directed her footfalls to the stable instead of the gardens in search of Gwen. An ancestor with a sensitive nose planted spruce trees between the house and stable to keep the odor of horses and their effluvium away from the house. As Clarissant rounded the grove, pungent pine fragrance died beneath the aromas of horse, leather and what would make grand fertilizer for her garden. The murmur of male voices grew clear as she drew close to the door, Tristan's clearest of all.

"Yes, they are a fine team. Bought them at Tattersalls and drove them down this morning."

He'd driven down from London that morning? He must have started before dawn. No wonder the horses looked lathered upon arrival and one suffered swelling.

The groom, a long-time family retainer who'd known Tristan since boyhood, expressed similar sentiments. He sounded disrespectful, but Tristan only laughed.

"A wasted journey, anyway." Despite the laugh, Tristan sounded sad.

Clarissant's heart squeezed as though a fist clenched around it. She stepped into the doorway, intending to announce her arrival before Tristan said more that could wound her.

Then she heard the carriage wheels on the drive. Rumbling wheels. The sound of a heavy vehicle tooling toward the house. She didn't need to turn around to know to whom the carriage belonged.

She turned around anyway. Behind her, the men's conversation ceased. Footfalls scraped on the sandy floor, and she sensed a presence behind her. The stable smells masked the man's scent, but she knew Tristan stood behind her. He didn't speak. She couldn't speak. Dryness closed her throat.

The carriage swept up to the front steps and stopped. Gray horses with platinum manes and tails dropped their heads in fatigue, and a coachman in gray and silver livery leaped from the box. A footman alighted from the other side and rounded the vehicle to open the door and lower the steps for his mistress. Trees masked that sight from the stable doorway, but the blue and silver Seasham crest glowed on the nearside panel, announcing who had arrived.

Tristan's journey from London was not completely wasted. Rowena had arrived at Bedevere Park.

Chapter Four

If possible, Rowena was more beautiful than she had been six years earlier. Her skin, always fine, glowed with blooming health, and her hair had darkened from lemon to pure gold. Sapphires shimmered at her ears, seeming to draw their color from the brilliance of her eyes.

From the shadow of the stable, Tristan took in her perfection, then remembered with a tightening of his chest that she was now married, and looked away. He should walk away . . . and keep walking, remove himself from this heartache. But he needed to talk to her. And he must remain for Gwen's come-out. Whatever the pain to his heart, he couldn't let his sister down.

Deciding he must face Rowena if he was to get through the next two weeks, he stepped into the sunlight.

Rowena's eyes widened, her face paled, and she pressed both beringed hands to her heart. *No!* Her begonia-pink lips formed the word, but no sound emerged. She swayed.

Tristan reached out to catch her if she fainted, but she did not. She drew back her arm and slapped him across his face.

His hand flew to his cheek. "What in the—"

Behind him, a footman let out a low whistle. The butler holding open the front door stared with wide eyes and open mouth.

"You let me think you were dead." Apparently unaware of the gaping servants, Rowena stepped closer to Tristan. Her eyes blazed, and she raised her hand again. "Not one word—"

"Rowena." Clarissant appeared beside her sister and caught her wrist. "Have your quarrel in private, not in front of the servants, unless you want Mama to hear of it and go into a spasm right before we're due in London."

Rowena turned her flashing eyes on Clarissant. "And a fine sight you'll make with your face all swollen. What *have* you been doing to yourself? Mixing potions . . ." She snapped her teeth together and bowed her head. "You're right. Not in front of the servants. It's the shock. Tristan . . . will you forgive me?" She raised her face to him and gave him the smile that had always melted him.

It melted him now despite his stinging cheek—or perhaps because of it.

He bowed over her extended hand. "Of course I do. But don't blame Clarie for her face. She went and got herself stung by a bee over the shock of seeing me."

Rowena's laughter trilled like a nightingale's song. "She is such a hoyden, playing in her garden like Marie Antoinette. So charming is my little sister."

"She always has been charming." Tristan glanced to

see Clarissant's reaction to this discussion of her attributes, but only caught a glimpse of her lavender gown disappearing around the corner of the house.

Rowena's eyes grew sad. "A pity she couldn't leave us alone when she was a child. She's learned discretion, now that it's too late."

Tristan flinched at the last two words. *Too late. Too late. Too late . . .* Hammer blows to his heart.

"How could you do it, Rowena? How could you wed another man?" Anguish rang in his voice.

The footmen behind him cleared his throat. "Aught I take your bags into the house, milady?"

"Well, of course you should." Rowena turned toward the house. "I'd like some lemonade and simply must get out of the sun. Tristan, come into the parlor with me, and you can explain what kept you away so long."

Tristan hesitated. He'd been away from the civilities of society for such a long time, he didn't know the protocol of a single gentleman enjoying a *tete-a-tete* with a married lady. He thought that Londoners accepted it, but this was the country, and this was the home of his parents' dearest friends—his dearest friends too. He wished to do nothing that would shame either them or himself, and especially not Rowena.

"Miss Moss has just released Lord Monmouth from the schoolroom," the butler said to Tristan as Rowena vanished into the parlor. "I'll have her join you."

Tristan let out a breath of relief. "Thank you. I do wish to talk to—" He stopped himself from explaining himself to a servant, though he didn't know why he should. With a nod to the butler, he started to follow

Rowena, and then paused. "Do you know the where-abouts of my sister, Jamison?"

"Miss Apking left the house an hour ago, sir, and I haven't seen her since. Shall I send her in if she returns?"

"Please do." Tristan took another step toward the parlor, then paused again. "Should I ring for refreshments, or will you send for them?"

"I believe Lady Seasham has already rung, sir." Was that a hint of amusement in the butler's voice?

Of course it was. Tristan was making a cake of himself and knew it. Yet he felt reluctant to meet Rowena in the parlor until someone else joined them. Did he fear what he would say to her? Or what she'd say to him? No reason for it. He had the answer he needed, however painful that was. She thought he was dead. None of his letters ever reached her. She was a lovely lady. Of course she wed . . . what kind of man?

That was why he needed to talk to her. He needed to give himself the peace of mind of knowing that she married well, not for just a title and money to save her family from poverty.

He stepped into the parlor, simply yet elegantly furnished with delicate tables and chairs and not the shabby, scarred sofas he'd known from before. As delicate as one of the figurines on the mantel, Rowena stood before an open window where the sunlight created a halo of her hair. Tristan walked to the opposite side of the room to lean against the chimneypiece with one foot on the cold hearth.

"I'm certain my father intercepted your letters to me," Rowena blurted out. "I know you would have written. The only word we had after you left was that your ship went down with all hands lost except a few who were captured." She took a step forward. "Were you captured? Have you been in a French prison all these years?"

"No, I've been aboard a merchant trader." Though he knew doing so was vulgar, he added, "I've been making that fortune I promised you if you waited for me."

Rowena clenched her fists. "I couldn't know that. You went into the Army of all things. Who makes his fortune in the Army? And I was weary of being stranded in the country. Seasham . . ." She turned and glided across the Wilton carpet to perch on the edge of a Chippendale chair with gold silk cushions that matched her hair. "Do sit down, Tris."

He remained standing. "Is he a good man? Do you love him, Rowena?"

"Of course I love him," she snapped. "What a rude question. Why would I marry a man I didn't love?"

"To save your family." He heard footfalls in the hall and knew he may as well speak his piece now, for he would never give himself another chance. "I can bear losing you forever if I know your heart didn't turn from me on a whim."

Rowena's lips tightened, paled. "Well, of course it didn't. We were wretchedly poor with no prospects of matters getting better. Father's man of business had stolen from us. We owed taxes and wages to the servants . . . Seasham saved me from all that . . . and helped Clarie too." She waved a hand in the air, diamonds flashing. "See how pretty this room is now? Remember how it was six years ago?"

"Yes." Some of the pain eased from around his heart.

He'd heard it from Rowena herself—her family needed help in a desperate way. Clarissant had been too young to marry, so Rowena sacrificed her own wishes to marry a man who would support them all.

And she thought you were dead.

The parlor door opened, and Miss Moss bustled in. "Rowena, you're early for once. Did you bring the children?"

Clarissant made a circuit of the terrace and returned to the house in time to hear Tristan's and Rowena's conversation through the open parlor window. The relief that rang in his single "Yes," warned her that Rowena had convinced him of her self-sacrifice in marrying Tom Hornwick, Lord Seasham.

"Lying cat," Clarissant muttered, then chastised herself for saying such a thing about her sister.

Clarissant knew that she wasn't the only person capable of not telling Tristan the truth to spare his feelings. Mossy wouldn't. Neither would Gwen. So why wouldn't Rowena have the same motive in glossing over the way she had married Seasham mere months after Tristan left Surrey, and even less time after they received word Tristan's ship went down?

Because Rowena needed everyone to love her. Everyone did—including Tristan.

Tears glazing her vision, Clarissant stumbled away from the window as Miss Moss made her entrance. How Tristan would react to the announcement of children— badly done by Mossy—Clarissant didn't want to know.

Besides, she had work to do. If she hurried and commandeered a couple of the maids, she could get the violets picked in time to press them for their perfume oils. She would lose much of it because of the advanced hour, but wouldn't need to purchase quite so much. Of course, she always purchased the oils for the factory. In no way could Monmouth grow enough flowers to support the business. Clarissant used what she grew and collected on the estate for her experiments. "Her little hobby," as Mama called it.

Mama had no idea what Clarissant's "little hobby" purchased; luxuries like the silk gown, and cushioned divan on which Mama reclined in the shade on the side terrace, and the chocolate in her porcelain cup.

Clarissant paused at her mother's feet. "You're awake early, and about?"

Mama smiled at her. "The doctor said I must take advantage of fresh air on fine days like this one, so here I am. I must admit it is lovely, and the flowers are so peaceful. Did I hear Rowena arrive?"

No comment on Tristan's arrival? Could she possibly not know?

Clarissant trod carefully. "Yes, Rowena's here. She's distressed with me because I have a bee sting that's swelling up my face."

Mama raised her head. "Heavens, I didn't even notice. Do you think a poultice will bring it down in time for the London journey?"

"A lavender wash will do, or perhaps evening primrose oil." Clarissant touched a fingertip to the throbbing puffiness. "I can always sit out the ball and allow Gwen to have all the attention."

"Nonsense. You must find a husband, too, great girl that you are now. What are you? Twenty?"

"And three, Mama."

Mama let out a little shriek. "Never say so. If we must, we'll add more ruffles to your gown to make you appear younger."

Clarissant suppressed a groan. More ruffles—any ruffles—would make her look a quiz, not a green girl.

She started to make an excuse to go on her way, then knew she had to mention Tristan's return so Mama didn't suffer too much of a shock and have one of her heart spasms.

She took a deep breath. "Mama, have you heard word of our other visitor this morning?"

"My maid said something about an old family friend returning." Mama waved a pale hand in the air as though erasing a slate. "But you know how Becker is. She's so new here, she knows no one and doesn't try to, so she reports absolutely nothing important to me."

The maid—another luxury—was more a companion, being well-educated and not one to gossip. Clarissant found this admirable. Mama found it boring.

Clarissant took her mother's hand in both of hers. "This may be a shock to you, Mama, but I must tell you that Tristan Apking is not dead. He returned this morning looking quite prosperous and . . . and . . . Mama?"

Mama sat upright, her eyes wide, her lips parted in laughter. "Now I don't need to worry about you not finding a husband. With Rowena safely wed, you can marry Tristan."

"No, Mama, I cannot."

"Of course you can. You always wanted to." Mama clapped her hands. "This is marvelous news, more strengthening than this fresh air. I won't have a daughter on the shelf after all."

"But, Mama—"

"No arguments. Run along and make yourself as pretty as you can. I must make certain those gowns you ordered are acceptable."

Certain she was the one who would suffer heart palpitations, Clarissant allowed her mother to amble back to the house without hearing any of the dozens of protests rising to Clarissant's lips. Mama wouldn't find the gowns acceptable, and not enough time remained for her to damage any of them with sprays of ribbon on the shoulders or extra flounces of lace around the hems.

But what could Mama do with Tristan if she had it in her head that he should marry Clarissant?

Her insides quaking with too many possibilities there, Clarissant headed for the kitchens. She found two maids the cook could spare, tossed a smock over her gown, and led the way to the trees she'd kept standing to shade the delicate blossoms of the violets. Because of the shade the flowers still held their purple heads high, promising considerable amounts of oil for her work, though not as much as she'd like.

Flat baskets balanced on their shoulders, Clarissant led the maids to her workshed to begin the delicate process of extracting the oil from the flowers. As they worked, the maids chattered about a gathering they'd attended the night before, and Clarissant wondered how she could proceed with her work while in London. She did not want to go. Even less did she want to go now that Tristan would be there, possibly joining the entourage of gentlemen who followed Rowena around. Fashionable or not for married ladies to have their courtiers like troubadours of six hundred years ago,

Clarissant didn't approve. Leave the single gentlemen for the single ladies.

But Tristan never had been for Clarissant.

She sighed. Over the maid's chitchat, she heard trill laughter and a masculine voice rumbling in response. She recognized the source of the feminine mirth— Gwenevere. But the man? Tristan's voice had certainly deepened, and had it deepened that much? More than likely. Now Gwen would hear all of his stories while Clarissant worked at flowers she could no longer smell, for violets, when sniffed too long, numbed the nostrils. Preferring jasmine, she never wore violet scent herself. She left that for Rowena—delicate and elusive with short-lived beauty.

Clarissant gave herself a mental pinch. No fair being such a cat toward her sister. Rowena made little effort to attract all the males to her. They caught one glimpse of her perfect complexion and golden curls and dropped at her feet like overfed flies.

And that is unkind to men.

Clarissant sighed. Normally, she wasn't so uncharitable. Now, with Tristan returned and still enamored of Rowena, she found herself biting her tongue against snapping at the maids or running outside to demand why Gwen hadn't waited for her to hear Tristan's tales of his adventures. They were to blame for nothing in their actions.

Her heart just hurt so much!

The violets ready for steeping, Clarissant dismissed the maids and closed and locked the workshed. She would go to her workshop for a while and miss dinner. If anything could soothe her heart, the cure—or at least the treatment—lay in experiments that produced fragrances delicate enough for a young lady newly launched into society, to heavy enough for an elderly matron to smell as her senses grew dim with age. Lately, Clarissant had been working on novelty items such as ink scented the same as her perfumes. She'd written several sheets with the different fragrances to see if they needed adjustment to make them stronger or weaker, how many drops of perfume oil per ounce of ink, and how long the scent lasted on a paper. She would inspect her inks and make the proper calculations that day, while everyone else was occupied with Tristan. He wouldn't miss her. He had Rowena and Gwen.

Her heart as heavy as a cask of perfume, Clarissant rounded the line of outbuildings to the entrance of her workshop and saw Gwen not with Tristan, but with Ian McLean, her man of business.

They didn't even acknowledge Clarissant's approach, as they stood before the building talking and laughing. With the sun shining on her hair, turning the deep red to a striking garnet hue, and her face alight with joy, she looked outright beautiful.

Ian, a stately Scot with nearly gypsy-dark features, never smiled. He worked hard running Clarissant's factory and pretending to be the man of business for the estate, and she had never seen him smile. But he smiled now, as he gazed down at Gwen.

Clarissant felt sick. She shouldn't. Gwen and Ian were both unattached and free to flirt with whomever they chose. Yet sight of their camaraderie left Clarissant realizing how much of her life she wasted on a man who would not—could not—ever care for her.

So the London journey would be worth it. She could find a husband and set her mother's mind—easily agitated at best—at ease, provide her brother with a father since Rowena had taken no interest in him, and find a way to finally forget about Tristan.

And my business?

Conscious that a husband would more than likely insist she dispose of the perfumery because of how it would ruin her reputation—not to mention his and both their families'—Clarissant rebelled again at the idea of marriage. That perfumery was important to her. It lifted the Behns out of abject poverty to respectable prosperity. It gave her something to do besides read Minerva Press novels and browse through *La Belle Assemblée*. It was her brainchild, her creation, her life.

If Gwen became too friendly with Ian, she might learn that he was not Clarissant's man of business for the estate. Gwen would never intend to tell anyone and ruin Clarissant's reputation for being in trade, but she would forget one day and blurt it out.

No, Clarissant could not allow them to be friends— or more. Especially not more. Ian had no fortune of his own and depended on Clarissant's business succeeding and continuing to flourish for his own livelihood, and Gwen would bring her husband only a small dowry. The *ton* would not like one of its own smelling of the shop, however pleasant the aroma in perfume oils, so exposure would compel the ladies of the *haut ton* to patronize other businesses. Clarissant would lose the income she needed to support her family and continue improving the estate back to prosperity, and Ian—what would he do?

No, Gwen must marry wisely.

Clarissant trod heavily on the gravel path leading to her workshop so that the stone crunched and rattled to announce her approach. "Mister McLean, have you brought me those accounts?"

Ian jumped, a guilty expression tightening his features. He stiffened, and half-raised his hand as though about to salute.

So she'd been a bit harsh in her tone, but doing so was for the good of all of them.

"I've put them in your office, ma'am." His Scottish accent sounded thicker than normal.

"Then why are you not in there with them?" Clarissant despised her imperious tone, and, again, couldn't help it.

Gwen turned on her. "He was kind enough to help me find an earring I lost on the path."

"What were you doing on this path?" Clarissant's alarm that Gwen had been snooping in her workshop gave her voice a shrewish edge. "You should be with your brother."

Gwen grimaced. "He's with Rowena. He's not interested—"

"And neither is Mister McLean." Clarissant shot Ian a pleading glance past Gwen's shoulder, hoping he'd understand why she'd just pointed out that he was an employee, not a family member. He held his mouth in a hard, thin line, which didn't bode well for his understanding her sharpness, so she added more gently, "Please, Gwen, Mister McLean and I have tedious business to discuss. Will you go interrupt your brother and Rowena's *tete-a-tete*? Miss Moss was with them, but . . ." She shrugged.

Gwen looked mutinous.

Clarissant grasped her hand and tugged. "Please, for your brother's sake. You know Rowena still wants everyone to love her, even if she is wed. It may all be innocent, but I don't like it."

From the corner of her eye, she saw Ian flush. He, too, had succumbed to Rowena's machinations, talking to her each time their paths crossed, until Clarissant threatened to dismiss him if he didn't stop dangling after Rowena.

"There is a matter or two I wish to discuss with you, Miss Behn," Ian murmured. "That order of . . . er . . . whale oil."

Whale oil? Clarissant stared at him blankly, then realized he really meant ambergris, from the insides of whales and used in making perfume.

"Not trouble with delivery, I hope?" Clarissant's concern was genuine.

"No, ma'am, merely the cost. I'm trying to bargain—"

"All right, I'm off." Gwen flounced up the path, drawing Ian's eye.

"Ian," Clarissant said with the warmth she normally displayed to the man who was as much a friend as business associate, "Gwen isn't for you."

"Nay, but she's a bonnie lass." He sighed, then turned to open the workshop door, releasing a potpourri of lavender, violet, jasmine, and rose into the warming day. "I willna talk to her again if I can avoid it."

Clarissant preceded him into the dim chamber with its shelves of bottles and jars of oils and petals, purified alcohol and water. Her nose twitched at the scent of something going bad, a scent spoiling in its container because she'd done something wrong in the mixing. She sighed, hoping it wasn't the ink. She had such hopes for that product to be sold in decorative bottles every lady would want gracing her writing desk. "You won't be able to avoid seeing her once we're in London. Just make certain you don't lose your heart to her. It'll do no one any good."

" 'Tis too late for that warning, Miss Clarissant." Ian gave her a sad smile. "I a'ready have."

Chapter Five

"**Y**ou'll be the belle of the ball," Gwen informed Clarissant, as they placed the final touches on their toilette for their come-out ball.

Clarissant dabbed a pinch of rice powder on her nose to minimize a slight sunburn she'd received in the park the day before, and grimaced at her reflection in the mirror. "My dear friend, I'm not even on the flight of fashion, let alone the first stair."

"Don't be absurd." Gwen stepped to the middle of the bedchamber they shared in Rowena's townhouse, and performed a pirouette on the toes of her white kid slippers. Her white gauze and satin ball gown flowed around her like rising mist, and candlelight glinted red in her dark hair.

Clarissant sighed with a twinge of envy. "You, my dear, are most definitely a diamond of the first water."

Gwen planted her hands on her hips. "You cast me in the shade. If only I had your height and—" She gestured in front of her to indicate Clarissant's voluptuous endowments. "And don't make faces like that. What if your face froze that way?"

"I'd gain more attention than I've garnered since our arrival here last week." Clarissant tried to keep her tone light.

Gwen's frown warned her that she'd failed. "Have you not noticed how the gentlemen stare at you when we've been out driving? You're stunning. You're Juno and Venus and Minerva and Diana and—"

"More like Ceres."

"Who?"

Clarissant tut-tutted. "Don't let Mossy hear you not knowing your mythology. Ceres is the earth mother, the goddess of corn to the Romans."

"Oh?" Gwen's winged brows swooped toward her hairline. "Matronly." She giggled. "Then you should marry."

Clarissant wished she felt that way. She wished that, in the sea of humanity that would soon arrive at the Grosvenor Square mansion, she would find a man who would turn her heart from Tristan. That would make the London visit and expense bearable. Thus far, since their arrival a week ago, she had met no one who even interested her beyond someone with whom she could spend a pleasant five minutes engaged in small talk.

Not that Tristan and she talked all that much. He seemed determined to avoid her, taking Gwen out for drives and even on shopping excursions, but avoiding Rowena's house or any of the social events she or Clarissant attended.

Which is for the best.

Clarissant turned her thoughts from Tristan and smoothed a hand down the simple ivory silk gown trimmed with gold embroidery at the hem, neck, high waist and short, puffed sleeves. Her mother declared it boring, but even Rowena approved Clarissant's choice.

"She's too robust to fit out in ruffles and flounces," Rowena said. Her own gown in peach and silver possessed a number of these. "And the fuller skirts minimize her height."

Translation: my sister is an Amazon.

So she favored their father rather than their mother. At least she had more business sense than either of them, and the family wasn't living in abject poverty on a corner of the estate while someone rented their house.

And I'm being a cat.

Giving herself a shake that threatened to topple her coronet of curls, Clarissant pasted on a smile and tried to mince rather than stride to the door. "Shall we make our *grande entrance*?"

"Oh, yes." Gwen gave a little skip, then stopped, squared her shoulders, and glided to the door with the grace of a swan on a serene lake.

Judging from the lack of light or sound coming from beyond closed bedchamber doors, everyone except Rowena had already descended to the lower floor to begin the receiving line for the imminent arrival of the guests. Laughter drifted up the stairs—Mossy's low chuckle, Mama's girlish trill, Seasham's bass rumble, Tristan's voice, lower than tenor, not quite baritone.

Clarissant's stomach knotted. She should have taken the light refreshment Mossy recommended, but she'd just returned from a walk in the park while the other ladies napped, and the smell of drains had left her feeling unwell. At least she told herself it was the smell of the drains and not anxiety over the ball. She was never nervous about anything except for the profits of her business and unexpected expenses. So why would she be nervous about this ball? She'd attended two soirees already with nothing untoward occurring. Of course, she'd been a nobody, a country mouse dragged about by her dazzling elder sister and sparkling friend. Now she was a guest of honor, someone with whom gentlemen would feel obligated to dance.

Like Tristan?

Gwen grasped her arm. "Don't fall down the stairs."

Clarissant halted. She did indeed stand at the top of the steep steps—carpeted at least—and her next step would have carried her into space.

She caught hold of the banister, momentarily dizzy. "Th–thank you."

Gwen giggled. "Are you, of all people, nervous?"

"I must be."

Below on the brightly lit landing, heads turned and gazes lifted. Mossy nodded with approval. Mama frowned for an instant, then smiled. Seasham grinned with his open warmth.

Tristan looked . . . disappointed.

Clarissant's eyes burned. Apparently, he didn't like what he saw in her or his sister's appearances. Or was the disappointment merely because Rowena didn't accompany them. Surely he knew she would wait until they were all assembled to greet the guests before she made her grand entrance. Surely he knew better than to pine after a married lady. Surely—

Gwen poked her in the back. "Go down. I hear a carriage rolling up."

Clarissant heard it, too, the sound of the first guests arriving. No doubt Rowena would hear it, too, or her maid would alert her to the arrival. She would want to appear in time for as many persons as possible to admire her. Since Rowena was usually something worth admiring, Clarissant lifted her skirt a mere inch off the floor and descended the steps with the firm tread of a body on a mission.

Was she truly considering finding a replacement for Tristan? An absurd notion. She was only in London because Gwen insisted she join her. Clarissant, a noblewoman in trade, could not marry anyone and allow him to, by law, take over the business that supported her family. He'd probably shut it down to preserve the family name, and if he weren't wealthy enough to support Monmouth, too, her family would suffer.

So she could find a husband—if he were wealthy. Rowena would certainly try to find Clarissant a husband.

Seasham, her brother-in-law, greeted her first, clasping her gloved hand between both of his. "You, my dear, are stunning. You won't stay on the shelf looking like you do."

"She shouldn't be on the shelf at all," Mossy declared, "and well you know it, my lord."

"If I'd had my way."

"No, my dear," Seasham said, tilting his head back, "yours did."

Clarissant followed his gaze up to where Rowena appeared at the top of the stairs like the radiance of sunrise after a gray dawn. A glance back to her brother-in-law showed her that his face radiated with pride, joy, and love.

Her heart constricted with the disreputable sense of envy. Did Rowena appreciate what she had, or did she want more, as she always had?

Like pressing on a bruise to see how painful it was, Clarissant glanced at Tristan to observe his reaction to Rowena. To her astonishment, he wasn't looking at her. He stood with his hands on Gwen's shoulders and his gaze firmly fixed on her face. They were laughing at a private joke.

Clarissant backed up to the wall at the top of the next flight of stairs, waiting for the others to cross the landing to her and the guests to ascend. She wondered if any wallflower grew her size. What was that huge plant called, the one the Russians were starting to grow to take oil out of its seeds? The sunflower. That was it. She was like a sunflower—too big not to be noticed, and useless unless someone squashed her.

That notion made her smile just as Ian McLean reached the top of the stairs. Apparently, the butler hadn't found announcing the arrival of the man of business necessary when other guests were ascending the front steps.

Ian met Clarissant's gaze and nodded to her. "You are in looks tonight, Miss Behn, if a lowly . . . er . . . businessman is permitted to say so." He bowed over her extended hand.

Flattered despite knowing he was merely being polite, Clarissant felt her cheeks warm. "You're permitted tonight, I believe, thank you. Do make yourself at home here."

"I've come to ensure the orchestra is behaving itself." Ian glanced at Seasham. "His lordship asked if I would do so, as I ken a wee bit about music."

"I never knew you—" Clarissant stopped, noticing that Ian had turned his attention to Gwen, though he nodded to Seasham and bowed to Rowena before slipping into the ballroom.

So the lecture she'd given him about how Gwen could not marry a man without means had done no good. Why had she thought it would? Her heart drew itself to Tristan despite her stern lectures to it to only care for him as a friend.

If only he were at least that . . .

No time to dwell on Tristan. From the entryway below, the butler motioned for the family to line up for receiving their guests. Mossy excused herself to oversee the refreshments, and the first arrivals ascended the staircase. Couples, single gentlemen and mothers—rarely with the fathers—with their daughters and sometimes sons in tow, flowed past like an uphill stream. Wedged between Seashham and Gwen, Clarissant smiled, nodded, and surreptitiously nursed fingers crushed from too many hand squeezes. The heelless kid slippers began to make her feet ache. The corners of her lips quivered from holding a smile too long.

"How many more people can arrive?" Gwen whispered in Clarissant's ear.

"Only three hundred and ninety-eight so far," Clarissant responded from behind her smile. "Rowena invited five hundred."

"We can go in now," Rowena announced, slipping her hand into the crook of her husband's elbow. "The most important personages have arrived."

Gwen heaved a sigh of relief. "I won't have the strength to dance."

"As if anyone will ask you." Tristan tweaked one of the curls laying artistically over one shoulder, and smiled at her with a warmth that melted Clarissant's heart.

Of all the details she recalled about Tristan, how much he adored his younger sister was one she'd forgotten. The evidence before her made her love him even more.

She swallowed back a lump in her throat and walked alone to the ballroom behind Seasham and Rowena, Tristan and Gwen. About to enter the ballroom like a serving maid behind her employers, Clarissant considered bolting. But she'd spent all this money on her gown, so she may as well be seen in it—if anyone would notice her. If she could fall in love with someone else . . .

With her gaze on Tristan's broad, straight back and glossy deep red hair still too long for fashion, she didn't notice Ian until he touched her arm. "It's presumptive of me, Miss Behn, but I'm thinking you'd prefer me to no escort at all."

"Ian!" She could have hugged him, but their business friendship didn't stretch that far. So she settled for a pat on his arm. "Thank you. Did Mossy send you?"

"Nay, 'twas my idea, though I did ask Miss Moss if she thought it proper enough." He offered her his elbow.

As Clarissant took it, she noticed both Gwen and Tristan casting her backward glances with raised eyebrows. The notion that they might think she had an affection for Ian or him for her amused Clarissant. She could do far worse. But in the four years she'd known him, he never once gave her heart the slightest flutter.

And he loved Gwen. All the way into the ballroom, Clarissant noticed that Ian's gaze followed Gwen.

Clarissant tried not to watch Tristan then or for the next two hours of the ball. She danced with Seasham and with a succession of eligible bachelors and widowers from ages one and twenty to three times that; all, she suspected, Rowena's choices sent to keep the plain younger sister from being a wallflower at her own coming-out ball. By the supper dance, her feet were sore more from partners treading upon them than from dancing. Clarissant envied the young ladies who spent most of the evening in one of the gilt chairs against the walls. No one had signed her dance card for the supper dance, for that partner would escort her into the dining room for the midnight repast.

Apparently no one cared to make small talk with her over lobster patties and trifle. Good. Her repertoire of chitchat ran out with the third dance.

"Isn't the weather fine for May?"

"Last night, we saw the most amusing play . . ."

"What do you think of the fireworks at Vauxhall? Are they worth the crush?"

All the while, overwhelmed with the reek of pomades and perfumes—some of them her own applied with too lavish a hand—she wanted to say, "Have you never heard of moderation?"

But that was unkind. Some people simply did not have as keen a sense of smell as hers. Had she even dabbed scent on her wrists that evening?

Under the pretext of giving her dance card a near-sighted scrutiny, she raised her hand so her wrist was no more than six inches from her nose. She should be able to . . . her nostrils flared. Yes, she had been a little too liberal with the jasmine blend.

Or perhaps they simply liked it the best too.

Clarissant wrinkled her nose at the quantity of other scents that assailed her. Fragrance was an art, a delicate—

"Are you making a face at the name written on your card," Tristan asked from beside her, "or the lack of names?"

"Perfume," Clarissant murmured.

Tristan smelled like sunshine and fresh air. How did he manage it? She'd never encountered a scent like that. No cologne at all?

"There are no names written on my card." She held up the gilded parchment dangling from her wrist on a gold silk cord.

The card swung to and fro, and Tristan caught it in his hand. "I don't believe you."

"Believe me. I speak the truth." Clarissant glanced around at the couples lining up on the dance floor, a pastel flower garden of fluttering gowns punctuated with the blacks and dark blues of male fashions. It was a lovely sight marred for her by the overabundance of perfume, so much so she wondered that the cloud didn't rise up and ignite on the hundreds of candles shimmering in their chandeliers. "No one wants to dance with a female who's taller than he is."

"I do."

"I'm not taller than you." She lowered her gaze. "Besides that, I don't believe you."

"What? That I wish to dance with you?"

"Or talk to me or walk with me or—" What was she saying? She pressed the back of her wrist to her lips, forgetting the dangling dance card. The gold cord slipped between her teeth like a horse bit, dry and bitter.

Did weavers treat silk with arsenic? No, alum.

With a sigh of relief, she dropped her arm to her side and glanced about for the nearest bolt hole. That Tristan started laughing didn't help. With the music not yet playing, his voice rang out above the chatter and politely moderated chuckles and titters of the guests. Heads turned their way.

"What's the jest?" Seasham called from his position at the head of the line with Rowena.

Rowena's eyebrows looked a fraction closer together than usual, as much as she allowed of an expression of disapproval to mar the perfection of her face.

Clarissant took a gliding step toward the nearest opening—a window. Could she jump from the upper floor without breaking something—like her neck?

Tristan caught hold of her hand. "She said if I asked her to dance she'd eat her dance card, so I asked her just to see her do it."

"Why you lying—" Those were the only words Clarissant managed between clenched teeth before the room erupted with laughter. Heat suffused her body so quickly she glanced up to see if the perfume cloud had indeed ignited on the candle flames.

Tristan tugged on her hand. "Come along, Clarie. Dancing the Roger de Coverley is much more amusing to me than scraping your remains off of the areaway."

She was going to kill him. She truly was. He barely deigned to speak to her the remainder of the week in

Surrey and all week in London, and now he dared make a cake of her in front of the entire ball. He was treating her like . . . his little sister.

Her eyes stung. The dancers and candle flames blurred. Wrenching her hand free, she turned her back on Tristan and the ball, and as the orchestra commenced she marched out of the ball room.

The instant the doors closed behind her, the click of the latch indiscernible above the soaring music and slap of feet on the wooden floor, Clarissant knew she'd acted like a little sister. At the least, she'd acted too little like the grown lady she was supposed to be. She would hear of it from Rowena, from her mother, from Mossy, from Gwen, from Tristan, from Ian . . .

Was her life not her own?

Of course not. In deed and responsibility, if not in anyone else's eyes, she was the family matriarch. Everyone counted on her to keep the family solvent and continue to grow the prosperity of the estate for her brother's sake. Acting childish did no one any good, least of all her. And now she couldn't return, at least not now.

Would Tristan come after her? Afraid he might and she'd forget about being grownup and do something ridiculous like dump a glass of lemonade over his head, she slipped down the hall, nodding to several footmen, and entered an anteroom that would allow her to slip into the ballroom from a curtained alcove. To her relief, no one else had taken refuge on one of the sofas, so she interrupted no *tete-a-tetes,* nor needed to offer anyone an explanation about her own precipitate arrival. The door into the alcove stood a few inches ajar, allowing strains of music to billow into the chamber. Humming the lively tune, she drew the door open and stepped into the alcove before she realized that the curtained space, unlike the anteroom, was not empty.

Chapter Six

Now why had he treated Clarissant that way?

Tristan leaned against the wall and watched the dancers, waiting for a movement when everyone's back would be toward him so he could slip from the ballroom and find her. She'd looked genuinely distraught, though he couldn't imagine why, and some of the things she'd said to him made him think she was annoyed with him.

Not that she had any reason to be. He'd been spending time with his sister, enjoying having money to spend buying her all the pretty things she deserved, showing her off to the *ton*—and avoiding the Seasham townhouse. Surely Clarissant understood that he needed to avoid Rowena. She was married—and a mother. He had no right to even look at her, let alone talk to her. He needed to forget he'd loved her once.

Rowena a mother!

Would he like her children? No doubt they were

cherubs, as lovely and sweet as she had been . . . still was, of course. He wished he didn't like her husband so much, yet how could one not like friendly and generous Tom Hornwick, Earl of Seasham? No wonder Rowena managed to set aside her vow to wait for Tristan forever for a man like Seasham. Added to her belief that Tristan was dead, her marriage was understandable.

Knowing she believed him dead helped ease the pain in Tristan's heart, but Rowena had years to get over caring for him. He'd had only two weeks to forget about loving her. So avoiding her until the ball seemed like the best course of action. That meant avoiding Clarissant too. Yet he intended to dance with her. A succession of partners kept him away until the supper dance. Then, when he had his chance to enjoy some of her always entertaining company, he embarrassed her literally to tears, though he couldn't work out why. Gwen never minded his teasing.

He glanced around the room, looking for Gwen. From a scapegrace child, she'd grown into a lady of grace and poise. He liked her company. So did many of the eligible bachelors, he'd noticed. He wondered which one had the privilege of dancing the supper dance with her.

But he couldn't find her.

Nowhere in the ballroom did Gwen dance. Nowhere along the walls did she sit or stand. Surely she wasn't foolish enough to go into the garden with a gentleman. Gwen possessed more sense than that. But where had she gone?

He glanced around the chamber again, and caught the flutter of curtains over one of the retiring alcoves.

Gwen wouldn't dare enter there with anyone except an appropriate chaperone—would she?

Wanting to make certain his faith in her was justified, he started for the anteroom just as a shriek rose above the music like a badly bowed violin string, and Clarissant tumbled face-first from the curtain.

"Clarie!" He rushed to her, remembering the time he'd watched her fall out of a tree. His heart pounded as, against logic, he imagined one of her arms broken. That would ruin her season, prevent her from finding a husband this year . . . upset Rowena.

He dropped to his knees beside her. "Clarie, are you all right?"

She nodded, but didn't move other than her lovely coronet of hair tumbling to the floorboards.

He touched a braid. "Give me your hand. I'll help you up."

A shudder rippled along her back, but she didn't move.

"Clarie." Apprehension knotting inside him, he decided this called for boldness, and grasped her shoulders to raise her to a sitting position.

She grasped his wrists and yanked his hands away. "Go . . . away." She sounded winded.

If only having the breath knocked from her by her fall accounted for her stillness, she was likely all right. But why had she fallen?

"Clarie, if you're hurt, I can fetch help."

From whom? Behind him, the music swooped and soared, and the dancers swept down the line two by two to enter the supper rooms. No one but the wallflowers and some chaperones seemed to notice Clarissant in an inelegant heap on the ballroom floor.

An elderly matron with a cane stomped up beside him. "Too much wine."

Clarissant pushed herself upright.

"Do you need some air, child?" Tristan stood and held his hand down to her.

This time, she accepted his assistance. "Yes, please." She glanced at the gathering crowd of unattached females. "I tripped and caught the handle of my fan in my middle." She held up the now broken sticks of her fan. "Please, go enjoy your supper."

"You'd be better off getting dressed again than getting air," one pinch-faced young lady spoke into the silence at the end of the dance. "You look terrible."

With her hair tumbling around her shoulders, her cheeks flushed—probably from embarrassment—and her eyes brilliant with an emotion he couldn't read, Tristan thought Clarissant looked anything but terrible. She looked . . . beautiful.

Beautiful? Clarissant? Little—well, not so little— Clarie?

Tristan shook his head, feeling a bit winded himself. Pretty, yes. She'd always been that. But beautiful? Surely not. Yet that word stuck in his head.

He needed fresh air too.

The last of the dancers vanished into the dining room, and the others began to trickle away, whispering and casting backward glances as they departed. Only the matron with the cane remained.

"Have you been drinking?" she demanded.

The corners of Clarissant's lips twitched. "No, ma'am, but if I told you the truth, you'd likely think I had been. Tristan?" She squeezed his hand.

He drew it into the crook of his elbow, and addressed the elderly lady. "I'll take her to her nurse."

Clarissant pinched his forearm.

He grinned. "Her companion, I mean. Miss Moss."

The matron nodded. "An excellent woman. She'll be in good hands there."

"Indeed I will be." When the matron thumped away, Clarissant added, "If I were going to her."

"You should, you know."

"Don't you start that nonsense. I'm going for some air before I do swoon."

"The day you swoon will be the day I eat my hat."

"Like I was going to eat my dance card?" She glanced down at her wrist, but the gold cord no longer graced her wrist.

He looked about on the floor, but saw no sign of it. "You'll likely miss the rest of the dancing anyway, will you not?"

"I certainly hope so. The rest of the season will suit me just fine. And when Rowena hears of this—" She drew in a deep breath and coughed. "Air."

"But I think—"

She tried pulling her hand free.

He laid his other hand over hers, holding it against his arm, and conceded. "The garden if you'll be warm enough."

"I'll be warm enough." She turned to the alcove. "Come this way. We won't be noticed."

Tristan supposed no one could quibble at the propriety of him taking Clarissant into the garden. They'd known one another most of their lives. All her life, actually. He remembered her as a mewling infant.

He would be related to her if . . .

He yanked the curtain to the alcove aside. "What were you doing in here?"

"Trying to return to the ballroom."

"You succeeded, though I admit it was an odd way to make a grand entrance."

"What happened was even odder." A tremor went right down to her fingertips beneath his. "Tris . . . there's a door leading down to the garden from here." She steered him through an anteroom and down a narrow passageway where steps led to a rear door intended for servants, judging from another hallway leading to what sounded and smelled like the kitchens, and the hooks bearing several plain cloaks. He snatched up one of them and swung it around Clarissant's shoulders, then opened the door to cool air sweet with pine and lilacs.

"Of course Rowena's garden doesn't dare not grow in spite of the London soot." Clarissant moved ahead of him down a path lit with flambeaux.

Following her, Tristan noticed the scent of her perfume for the first time, drifting back to him like the memory of a lonely night on a tropical island. He'd longed for the scent of English roses, but received frangipani, the red, night-blooming jasmine. The scent made him more homesick than ever. He missed the adventure of struggling against storms and battling pirates.

But he mustn't even think about the pirates in the Indian Ocean for fear he would slip up and mention them to a society that wouldn't approve of where he'd gotten his fortune. Let them think he'd gotten it in honest trade. He had gotten it honestly, just not politely.

But he could tell Clarie, could he not?

Clarie, yes, but this was Clarissant, a grown up lady, nearly a stranger. An odd thought when he kept reminding himself that he'd known her for three and twenty years, yet he'd left behind a child and returned to find a lady. She was so beautiful and—

And what was he thinking? She was Rowena's younger sister.

Clarissant paused beside a stunted pine tree and plucked off a few needles. Their pungent aroma blotted out the jasmine. Good. He could think more clearly now.

He strode forward so he could face her. "So tell me what happened."

"What?" She glanced up at him, looking a little dazed, as though her thoughts ran far away.

He tapped a finger on her chin. "You told me you'd explain why you came tumbling into the ballroom if I brought you out here. I did, so speak."

"Oh, that." She shook her head. "It was the oddest thing. I was trying to slip back into the ballroom—"

"We've established that already. You did slip back in . . . in a manner of speaking."

She raised her fist as though intending to punch him, then dropped it to her side again and raised her chin. "Are you interested or not?"

"Of course I'm interested." Gazing into her lovely face, her skin smooth and golden in the light of the flambeaux, he found himself interested in more than her story, and stiffened his spine against a desire to return to sea—at once. "Go on."

She looked down at the pine needles she continued to rub between her fingers, no doubt staining her gloves. "There's an anteroom, you saw. Some sofas for those wanting to escape the crush in the ballroom. And there's that curtained alcove that separates the rooms. I think they're for servants to wait or some such. There's one at the other end of the ballroom too. Anyhow, I stepped into it, and someone was in there peeking through the curtains."

"Isn't that what it's for?"

She glanced up, her hands clutching around the pine sprigs. "Yes, I suppose it is, but Tristan he pushed me."

"He what? Who?" Tristan headed for the house as though he had a chance at catching the man who would dare harm Clarissant.

She caught hold of his arm. "Wait. You'll never find him, and you'll make a scene."

"I'll find him if you tell me what he looks like."

"But that's just it. I can't. He pushed me before I got more than a glimpse of him."

Tristan scowled. "Well, what was the glimpse?"

Clarissant tapped two fingers on her lower lip for a moment, her eyes closed. "I don't know. I mean, he wasn't a big man, but he wasn't small either. Maybe my height and a bit broader, though not much."

"Which precisely describes half the men at the ball. Was there nothing else about him? His hair? His dress?"

"No, nothing like that, but . . ." Her fingers tapped harder. "He smelled like mildew."

Tristan stared at her. "You noticed his smell? You didn't see him long enough to notice his clothes or hair color, but you noticed his smell?"

"Of course I did. I'm—" She pressed her fingers to

her lips and turned away from him. "We need to return to the house, or we'll get no supper."

He lifted a tumbled curl from her shoulder. "You need to get your *toilette* repaired before you go anywhere."

"Oh!" Her hands flew to her disheveled hair. "I forgot. I must look a fright."

"No, Clarissant, you're beautiful." The words emerged before he could stop himself.

She faced him, looking as startled as he felt for admitting such a thing to a lady who was nearly as much a little sister to him as was Gwen. Her eyes were wide, dark and brilliant in the torchlight. Her lips parted, then pressed together, and she began striding up the path as though wishing to run away from him but not daring to lose that much of her dignity.

Tristan sighed. He couldn't figure females. When he treated her like a sister, she grew upset. When he engaged in a moment's flirtation, she looked nearly horrified. He couldn't win with Clarissant. She wasn't his sister. She was a lovely grown lady now.

And she was Rowena's sister.

Even if he was interested in her—which he was not—she was off limits for that reason alone. When Rowena had married to save her family from penury, how could he even consider more than a mild friendship with Clarissant?

Had he been considering more than that?

No, of course not. He intended to return to sea as soon as he found a ship sailing for the East, or perhaps America. He would make another fortune and perhaps even settle in a foreign land.

Pondering which he would prefer—India or

America—Tristan headed back to the house. He knew what India had to offer a man seeking his fortune, but the climate in America was more welcoming. Both had groups of people hostile to the English. That he was Welsh didn't matter to enemies of the British. Both had cities. At least he thought America had cities now. He'd met someone from New York who—

A female giggle brought his musings to an abrupt halt. He stopped, realizing that he'd turned down a side path instead of the walk leading to the house. Fewer flambeaux burned here, but enough light filtered through shrubs and trellises to show him a man and woman seated side by side on a bench, though not their faces.

He bowed. "I beg your pardon."

The lady gasped, sprang to her feet, and fled away from him.

He was doing well that night, sending two females running away from him. Had he always been that abhorrent to females?

"I didn't mean to frighten her," he said to the gentleman.

"'Tis of no matter, sir." That individual rose, bowed, and strode away. Peculiar behavior to say the least.

Many of the guests that night seemed to be acting oddly. Or was it the same gentleman who had pushed Clarissant? He was of average height and build. Tristan hadn't noticed whether or not the man smelled of mildew. Presumably not, for surely the lady would not have been sitting so close if he did.

Suddenly weary of social foibles, Tristan decided to return to the ball long enough to take his leave of his host and hostess and sister.

Gwen! He'd forgotten all about Gwen and the fact he hadn't seen her since well before the supper dance.

Gwen burst into the bedchamber so fast she ran into the maid pinning up Clarissant's hair, sending pins flying across the room and sending the maid and herself staggering in opposite directions. Clarissant's hair tumbled back over her shoulders, and she had to grasp the edge of the dressing table to stop herself from falling off the stool.

"What in the world happened to you?" Slowly, she turned to face her friend.

Gwen sagged against the wall. "I could ask the same of you."

"Yes, but I asked first." Clarissant nodded to the maid, who knelt on the floor picking up pins. "You may go."

"No," Gwen countered, "I need your assistance with my hair."

Clarissant stood. "Later."

The maid bobbed a curtsy. "I'll wait outside, miss."

Gwen blocked the doorway. "There's no need, and we're missing the dancing."

"Then stop wasting time arguing with me." Clarissant caught hold of Gwen's arm and drew her out of the doorway.

The maid fled, yanking the door closed behind her.

Gwen tried to free herself. "It's nothing to concern you."

"You run in here like the furies are after you, your hair all falling down, and you expect me not to care?" Clarissant paused long enough to breathe.

"And what happened to your hair?" Gwen's eyes flashed a challenge.

Clarissant sighed, knowing she would have to tell Gwen the truth if she wanted it in return. "Someone pushed me."

"What? Who? How? Where? I don't believe—"

Clarissant pressed her hand to Gwen's lips. "Quiet. We'll have Rowena up here in an instant, and she'll ring a peal over us that will make us deaf for days."

"But, Clarie, she needs to know you were insulted in her house."

"No, she doesn't."

"But she'll learn . . . something."

No doubt she would.

Clarissant brushed at a smudge of dust on the front of her gown. "I'll tell her I tripped. She thinks I'm clumsy anyway."

Tristan said she was beautiful.

A thrill ran through her at that memory. He'd looked dazed after he said it, as though realizing he spoke to her, not some other lady, and he had said it. Her, beautiful!

"Clarie?" Gwen tapped her on the cheek. "You expect me to believe someone pushed you, when you go all dreamy-eyed like that? What truly happened?"

Clarissant stiffened her shoulders. "I was pushed. You can ask Tristan."

"I shall." Gwen snatched open the door as if intending to march downstairs and do that very thing. Instead, she opened the portal to Rowena.

Her lips white and her eyes flashing, she marched into the bedchamber and banged the door closed. "What is the meaning of the two of you disappearing from your own ball? I have never been so embarrassed and humiliated and shamed in my life. How you can do this to me—" She yanked open the door again. "Liza, come in here and repair their appearances at once."

Trembling, the maid slunk into the room and cast Clarissant a pleading glance.

"Take Miss Apking first," Rowena commanded. "Miss Behn can do her own hair."

With Gwen at the dressing table and Clarissant sitting on the edge of the bed so she could see herself in the mirror beyond her friend and maid, Rowena continued her diatribe against their shameful, shameless, and altogether unacceptable behavior. Not until Rowena practically dragged them back to the ballroom did Clarissant realize that she still knew nothing about what Gwen had done.

Chapter Seven

Clarissant locked the bedchamber door and dropped the key into the pocket of her morning gown. "You're not leaving this room until you tell me who you went into the garden with last night."

"How do you know I was in the—" Gwen clapped a hand across her mouth, then rubbed her eyes. "You shouldn't wake a body like that, Clarie. I could tell you anything."

"Like the truth?"

"Like–like—" Gwen struggled to a sitting position. "I don't need to 'fess up to anything to you. You're not my guardian."

"No, I'm your friend." Clarissant leaned against the door in a decidedly unladylike fashion. "But I can go fetch Tristan and show him this." From her other pocket, she drew out a pink rosette she'd found while in the garden reading that morning. She had no certainty that the rosette came from Gwen's gown until her friend paled, then flushed, and pressed the backs of her hands to her cheeks.

"Where . . . where . . . ?" She bounded from the bed and snatched the silk flower from Clarissant's hand.

"Gwenevere, what were you doing in the garden?"

Clarissant feared she knew, but needed to hear it before she confronted the other person involved.

Gwen turned her back on Clarissant and slunk to the dressing table. "My feet hurt, and I could scarce breathe. He . . . all we did was sit on a bench and talk."

At least Clarissant could believe that. Gwen would do nothing shameful. Still . . .

"All you and who did?" she pressed.

Gwen sighed. "Ian. I mean Mister McLean."

Clarissant groaned. "I was afraid of that."

She'd thought better of her business manager. Did he still not understand the risks of an involvement with a young lady of the *ton*? He could ruin Clarissant and her business. That would mean her family, and Tristan would learn that Seasham didn't support them, and . . .

She must talk to Ian at once.

She turned toward the door.

"Clarie." Gwen's voice rang with concern. "I tell you the truth. We only talked. Then Tristan came along and I ran off before he saw it was me. So if you have a fondness for Mister McLean, you needn't fear that I'll form an attachment with him. I wouldn't do that to you."

"A fondness?" Clarissant nearly laughed aloud and denied Gwen's notion that Clarissant had a *tendre* for the Scot, and therein laid her distress over Gwen's actions at the ball.

But why should she deny it? If Gwen thought that

Clarissant wanted Ian for herself, she would cease tossing her cap for him. Then, if Clarissant warned Ian off again, nothing could go wrong with the secret of the business.

Oh, why had she gone into trade? Now it was forcing her to keep apart two people who might genuinely care for one another. Yet what choice did she have? Her family needed to eat and have a place to live. Her brother needed a future. Gwen would find someone else. Clarissant had noticed how many gentlemen found her attractive, and perhaps Tristan would increase her dowry with his newfound wealth.

Found? Earned? Stolen?

She shook her head against the latter notion and addressed Gwen without looking at her. "Ian and I have been friends for many years. He works for me—us. You should set your sights higher."

"If it'll make you happy," Gwen said, not sounding happy herself, "I'll try."

"Thank you."

Feeling like she'd just taken a bone away from a hungry puppy, Clarissant left the bedchamber and descended to the front hall. The butler informed her that the hackney she'd ordered had arrived. His disapproving look told her he did not like the idea of a young lady going off on her own and in a hired carriage. No one else would like it either, so she needed to drive to the factory, make her inspections, talk to Ian, and return before Rowena rose from her bed and prepared to receive the scores of afternoon callers. That gave her two hours, since most of the *haut ton* stayed abed until at least noon.

Clarissant's hackney drove through the streets unimpeded, and she arrived at the factory in half an hour. There, she ran into difficulties, for the driver refused to stay.

"I need to make my living, miss."

"But how will I return to Mayfair?" Clarissant protested.

He shrugged and cracked the reins over the back of his weary-looking horse.

Clarissant started to call out a command for him to halt, then decided she couldn't be that undignified in front of her employees, especially not Ian when she needed to speak seriously with him.

He stood in the doorway, the overpowering aromas of perfume wafting into a street that otherwise held the unpleasant odors of bad drains. In such quantity, the perfume fragrance held few pleasures either, which was why she kept her workshop in the country where the air was fresh. She wrinkled her nose at the scents.

Ian grinned. "The ladies who purchase your wares wouldn't like to come here, would they? We're processing a batch of that ink today. I'm thinking it'll be a fine seller." He bowed. "Do come in, Miss Clarissant. The smell's not so bad in my office."

"Thank you, but I'd like to make an inspection of the premises first."

Her nostrils twitching, Clarissant followed Ian around vats of scent, boilers, tables of jars of ingredients and the delicate bottles for the finished product. The workers, mostly women, wore caps covering their hair, huge aprons and cloths over their noses and mouths. They greeted her with their eyes or a raised hand and continued to work measuring, stirring, pouring. Every surface looked spotless. The only place that concerned Clarissant was the fires under the boilers.

"Can we not have a separate room for these?"

Ian shook his head. "Nowhere to build. We need more space as it is."

"Perhaps we should look into renting other premises."

"Aye, that would work. I'll see to it straight away." Ian opened the door to a small office at one end of the building. "May I make you some tea?"

"Thank you, no, I can't stay for long." Clarissant ignored the chairs in the room and moved behind Ian's desk. She didn't like being high-handed with him, but if her business failed, he would be out of work and be unable to support a future wife, let alone the family members he already assisted.

"The business is going well," she began. "You are an excellent manager."

He bowed. "Thank you. That I own shares in it gives me motivation to work hard to make certain we continue profitable."

Silently thanking him for the opening she needed, she took a deep breath. "Then we need to ensure it remains profitable by making certain that no one in society learns that I own this business. You are aware that that would ruin us, are you not?"

"Aye, ma'am, I am." His green eyes were wary now.

Clarissant clasped her hands together at the waist of her lavender pelisse. "Then I'm going to remind you once again that your . . . affection for Gwenevere Apking must cease at once."

A hint of color rose in Ian's high cheekbones. "Were that that were possible, Miss Clarissant."

"I know." Clarissant's throat tightened in sympathy. "Hearts are unruly things, Ian, and I speak to you as much as a friend as an employer. There's no future for either of you in pursuing an attachment. The only solution is to stay away from her as much as possible."

But had six years of separation from Tristan stopped her affection for him?

Her heart ached for Ian. She thought Gwen's heart was not yet engaged, but poor Ian had fallen for Gwen long ago.

"All you can do is try," she added.

"I shall try." He looked about to bow again.

Clarissant held up a staying hand. "Cease all this formality, please. You'll get a crick in your back."

He gave her a half-smile that didn't reach his eyes. "As long as you pay my wages . . ."

They couldn't truly be friends.

Clarissant sighed. "Perhaps I should sell the business and invest in property. Leasing is a proper business for the family of a viscount."

Alarm clouded Ian's eyes. "Not yet, I beg of you, Miss Clarissant. I'd like—" He flushed. "I'd like to make the purchase myself, and as of now, I cannot manage it."

Not in the least surprised by this, Clarissant asked, "When do you think you can manage what this business is worth?"

Ian shrugged. "The end of the year."

The end of the year, not the season.

Not until a burden seemed to slide from her like a

sodden cloak did Clarissant realize that she had feared Ian could purchase the perfumery sooner than later, and she would have no business to run. Oh, she could manage the properties, and she could not imagine finding as much pleasure in that as she did in creating scents and products in which to use her fragrances.

She smiled at Ian. "I won't sell it to anyone else—if I choose to sell at all. In the meantime, try to forget Miss Apking."

"Yes, ma'am." Ian bowed, then went to the door. "May I offer you a ride back to Mayfair? You'll never get a hackney."

Clarissant accepted the offer so she would return before the household stirred. On the way back to Mayfair, they discussed whether or not they should sell the perfumed ink in the usual shops, or if they should pursue other venues such as stationers. By the time they reached Grosvenor Square, they had decided to try selling the ink at one or two of the more popular stationers.

At the front door of the Seasham townhouse, Clarissant had to vie with several florists' boys to gain entry. The entire front hall looked like a florist's shop with ranks of flowers piled on every surface and lying in rows on the floor. Noting Rowena's and Gwen's names on a few of the cards she could read, Clarissant thought both would be pleased and flattered. She wondered why neither of them had descended to accept these accolades to their beauty, character, or whatever the admirers chose to praise with flowers. Surely they didn't expect the footmen to carry them all up, since the tributes from all but a chosen few would go to one of the hospitals.

When she reached the upper floor with no public rooms, Clarissant received her answer—Rowena and Seasham were engaged in a row, and Gwen, two house-maids, and a footman stood in the hallway outside the bookroom door. One look from Clarissant sent the servants scampering to their duties.

Gwen rose on her toes to murmur in Clarissant's ear. "Lord Seasham has sent for the children, and Rowena is having a tantrum."

Clarissant thought she might have a stroke. What was Seasham thinking to bring the children to London at the height of the season? And how would Tristan react when he learned that Rowena's babies were not in the least babies but ages four and five? Well, nearly five. Thomas, the Viscount Ripon, son and heir, would be five—

In two weeks.

Clarissant pressed her hands to her now roiling middle.

"Do you expect my son to be without either parent on his birthday?" Seasham demanded, pounding home the source of Clarissant's abdominal distress.

If Thomas celebrated his birthday in London, Tristan would learn that Rowena had married Seasham a mere three months after Tristan left for the Army, nearly a year before they learned that his ship had gone down with all hands lost. Hadn't Tristan lost enough without the added humiliation and pain of learning that Rowena hadn't even pretended to wait for his return?

"I don't want to announce to the world that I'm old enough to have a five-year-old son." Rowena sounded on the edge of tears. "I'm nearly six and twenty."

"And more beautiful than ever for being the mother of my children." Tom's voice had roughened with affection.

Gwen rolled her eyes. "She'll get her way, you watch."

"We shouldn't listen," Clarissant said.

Neither of them moved.

"So I want all of London to know that my nonpareil wife has blessed me with two handsome and sturdy sons."

"But, Seasham, I've so much to do. How can I plan a birthday party too? I have my sister and Gwenevere to launch."

"They're launched." Approaching footfalls sounded on the floorboards beyond the bookroom door. Gwen and Clarissant headed up the steps to their bedchamber. "Ask Miss Moss for her assistance." Seasham's voice rang loud and clear as he opened the door. "Or Clarissant's."

She paused at the landing and glanced back. He winked at her.

She blushed and swung around the banister to head up the next flight. How embarrassing to have her brother-in-law catch her eavesdropping as though she were three and ten, not three and twenty!

Ahead of her, Gwen giggled like a schoolgirl. The instant their bedchamber door closed behind them, she sobered. "Why didn't you tell me you were going driving with Mister McLean?"

"I wasn't." Clarissant remembered that she could keep Gwen and Ian apart if the former thought her friend had a fondness for the latter. Gwen hadn't seemed overset with the notion, so keeping them apart was not a bad action, was it?

"I went out for some . . . ink," Clarissant explained, "and the hackney didn't wait for me, so when I saw Ian, he offered me a ride back here."

"How convenient." Gwen curled her upper lip. "And you're a very bad liar, Clarie. Do we dare go downstairs again? I do wish to see if anyone sent me flowers."

"If anyone sent you flowers?" Clarissant laughed. "Gwen, you can start a perfumery with all the petals down there."

"As if I'd deal in trade." Gwen snatched open the door. "I may only be Welsh gentry, and only acceptable to society because my brother is a baron and my father was friends with yours, but I won't sink that low."

That was more proof she wouldn't allow an attachment between Gwen and Ian—Scots gentry to be sure, but a working man nonetheless.

Clarissant followed Gwen down to the largest drawing room, where Rowena sat amid a sea of bouquets reading cards and writing down who had sent what to whom. For all her careless ways with those who loved her, Rowena would never slight an admirer by not sending him a thank you note for his floral gift, even if that arrangement ended up in the servants hall or a hospital ward.

Rowena offered Gwen a brilliant smile. "You have fourteen bouquets, Gwenevere. You are such a pretty friendly girl, I knew you'd take." Her smile faded as she turned to Clarissant. "You only have three. How I will ever marry you off, I do not know."

"I'll marry myself off," Clarissant snapped, "when I'm ready."

Rowena emitted a delicate snort. "That will be never. Our poor mother having you on her hands the rest of her life, and dear little Dunstan. When he's old enough to marry, do you think his wife will want you around? Or should your brother have the expense of upkeeping the dower house?"

Clarissant gritted her teeth. *I'll upkeep it myself. Or if he builds one, it'll be with money I earned instead of finding a husband.*

In silence, she took the three bouquets from her sister and read the cards. One was from a widower with six children all at least as old as she and probably a couple older. Another was from an amusing gentleman who had height and quick wit to recommend him but barely a feather to fly with. Of course, a poor husband might not mind keeping on the perfumery.

She decided to wear his nosegay to the operas that evening, and opened the third card. It bore no signature, only the words:

In apology for pushing you.

Clarissant stared at the three pink roses so long the other ladies ceased inspecting their own tributes and gave her their full attention.

"What is it?" Rowena asked.

Gwen merely plucked the card from Clarissant's fingers. "Who pushed you?"

"I don't know."

"An accident, no doubt," Rowena said. "It was a delicious crush last night, was it not? And if I can get one of my protégées married off from that, I will have great consequence as a London hostess. Perhaps one day I'll even be a patroness of Almak's."

For once, Clarissant did not mind the least that Rowena grabbed the limelight for herself. She didn't like being reminded of those startling moments when the man pushed her face-first into the ballroom. She didn't want to remember the tenderness in Tristan's voice, nor him touching her hair. She needed to remember him treating her like Gwen.

But he thought she was beautiful.

"So you have a secret admirer." Gwen's gray–green eyes sparkled. "How shall he reveal himself? Or will he continue to send you anonymous tributes to your charms and—"

"Nonsense," Rowena broke in. "She will discard these flowers at once."

Clarissant had been about to do that, but Rowena's haughtiness made her decide to wear them that evening. Perhaps someone would reveal himself and she could ask why he pushed her down.

She tucked the nosegay into the waist sash of her gown, where the delicate pink petals contrasted nicely with the lavender satin.

"An admirer, Clarie?"

Clarissant started at the sound of Tristan's voice. She looked at him lounging in the doorway of the drawing room. She expected to see teasing amusement in his eyes. Instead, he looked sober, perhaps even concerned.

Suddenly, she felt flustered. She could have countered teasing. Solemnity set her off balance.

"What are you doing here so early?" Gwen demanded before Clarissant thought up a response.

Now the twinkle appeared. "I've come to inspect the hordes of suitors who'll darken this doorway today.

And none too soon to judge from this display of horti-culture here. Must protect you from fortune hunters."

Rowena laughed. "Gwenevere doesn't have a fortune to hunt. She's not as poor as I was, but I had to be aware of the limitations of her dowry, you understand."

Tristan bowed to her with a startlingly cool formality. "I am aware of what the limitations were, my Lady Seasham, but those financial strictures no longer apply."

"Tristan!" Gwen's hand flew to her lips beneath her widened eyes.

Rowena narrowed her blue eyes to mere slits. "I see." Her voice held a hard edge. "She's come into a windfall?"

"In a manner of speaking." Was that triumph in Tris-tan's expression? "I can provide for her and then some. She may marry a poor man if she wishes, as long as he is not a spendthrift or gambler."

"I see." Rowena stood and shook out her skirts. "Well, you may discuss suitors with your sister without my assistance then. I must dress before our callers arrive. This gown is a positive rag." In a gown Clarissant knew quite well Rowena had purchased no more than two months earlier, Rowena flounced to the door. She paused there to crook a finger at Clarissant. "Join me while I make my *toilette*."

Clarissant cast her sister an innocent glance. "Shall I advise you on your hair ribbons?"

Rowena shuddered, wafting a violet-and-rose-scented handkerchief before her face. "Heaven forfend that you should advise me on anything to do with my *toilette*. I wish you to plan Thomas' birthday party."

From the corner of her eye, she saw Tristan's hands

clench, and she wanted to shake her sister. Rowena was the one who had wronged Tristan. Why should she feel the need to punish him? Did she resent the fact that he had returned with the fortune that kept them from marrying in the past?

Pity for her sister pricked Clarissant's conscience, and she trailed after Rowena with lagging footsteps. She wanted to remain with Tristan, steal every moment in his company that she could. Yet she knew she must not. Even though she believed that Rowena cared for her husband as much as she cared for anyone beyond her own exquisite person, Clarissant knew her sister was harsh when hurt. Rowena had been harsh with Tristan. That was a clear signal to Clarissant that Tristan's triumphant return hurt Rowena as much as it annoyed her. So how much more would a relationship between Clarissant and Tristan hurt Rowena?

Perhaps, Clarissant thought with a sigh as she trailed up the steps behind Rowena, she should set her cap for Ian McLean. She would never have to concern herself with revealing her secret business to her husband, or having him shut it down for being trade. And she and Ian liked one another. That was more of a foundation than many social marriages boasted.

But Ian loved Gwen, whom he could never have, and Clarissant loved Tristan, whom she could never have.

Chapter Eight

Clarissant had never planned a birthday party in her life. Mama usually took charge of such social gatherings, but there in London, Lady Monmouth had found a circle of likeminded friends and Clarissant scarcely ever saw her parent. She consulted Miss Moss, who immediately offered to perform the planning herself.

"You don't have the time with all the balls and parties you're attending."

Clarissant pulled a rueful face. "I'd love an excuse to stay home now and again."

"Rowena wouldn't stand for it. She's determined to get you married off."

"She won't. Now, about the guest list—"

"Where did those flowers come from?"

"What?" Clarissant glanced down at the nosegay she still wore tucked into her sash. Her cheeks heated. "I forgot. A secret admirer?"

Mossy narrowed her eyes. "Not Mister Apking? Or Mister McLean?"

Clarissant widened her eyes with what she hoped was a look of innocence. "Why, Mossy, whatever do you mean?"

"Miss Clarissant." Miss Moss' voice held the warning note Clarissant had learned from childhood, which meant she'd better stop funning and give a serious answer. The problem was, none of her answers were straight. Tristan's return had twisted everything into knots. Ian deciding he was in love with Gwen only added glue that held those knots in place. And Clarissant couldn't confide in Mossy; she couldn't even tell her governess-turned-companion that she supported the family, including Mossy's wages and the fund Clarissant set aside for the day when the spinster would be too old to work, or simply wished to be mistress of her own life.

She, too, would lose all that if the truth came out.

Clarissant turned her back on Miss Moss and strode to the desk. When she uncorked the ink bottle, the delicate scent of lilacs permeated her bedchamber. "Isn't this nice? I found it in a little stationer's shop and—"

"Miss Clarissant, bite your tongue before you tell any more lies," Miss Moss commanded. "I know perfectly well where that ink came from. Your mother may choose to ignore the signs, and Miss Gwen hasn't been in society long enough to work it out, but I've known for years who supports the family."

"Oh." Clarissant shivered with apprehension, splattering ink onto a fresh sheet of foolscap. "Does anyone else?"

"Besides Seasham and your sister? No." Mossy's

voice gentled, and she crossed the room to stand behind Clarissant. "But you can't keep up this charade for long. When you marry—"

"I won't."

"Of course you will. You're very pretty and so charming, and you likely would have a sizeable dowry if you sold the perfumery."

"I'm also three and twenty, and I can't sell it yet. Ian wants to buy it, and . . . oh, Mossy, I want to go home." The last emerged rather like a wail, and she struggled to control herself. "I was so much happier before we came to London."

Mossy laid a hand on her shoulder. "Weren't you happier before Mister Apking returned from the dead?"

Throat closing, Clarissant nodded.

"Poor child." Mossy patted her shoulder. "You never did give up on him, did you?"

Clarissant shook her head.

"And he hasn't given up on Lady Seasham."

Clarissant nodded.

"Well then . . ." Mossy snatched up the ruined paper and laid out a new one. "The birthday party is the best news we have had all day."

Clarissant glanced up. "What are you saying? It's a disaster. Tristan will learn that Rowena never even waited to learn he was dead before she got married."

"Precisely. It's past time he learned the truth."

Tristan stood in the drawing room doorway enjoying the sight of his sister surrounded by admirers. The first callers had arrived before he managed to extract from her exactly to where she had disappeared during the ball the night before, but seeing her sparkle beneath the attentions of not one but four eligible bachelors made him shove that aside as insignificant. Gwen was happy and would more than likely end up at the least betrothed by the end of the season if not before. His brother was happily settled on his estate in Wales, prospering with the introduction of horse stock, and pleased with his marriage. Just that morning, Tristan had learned of a ship sailing for the new American city of New Orleans in a week's time. A merchant ship, it needed an experienced supercargo. Tristan was qualified. With his family apparently settled in their lives, he could sail with a clear conscience.

If not a clear heart.

Careful not to look in Rowena's direction, he stepped back from the doorway just as Clarissant sped down the stairs so light on her feet she scarcely made a sound in her kid slippers. Her lavender gown swayed and fluttered around her like morning mist, and three rosebuds clung to her waist.

Suppressing an irrational urge to snatch them out of her sash and stomp them into the carpet, Tristan gave her a half bow. "What's the hurry, Clarie?"

She started, missed the last step, and sat down hard on the lowest tread with a thud. "Heaven's, Tris." She pressed a hand to her chest. "You shouldn't lurk about scaring people."

"You shouldn't be running down the steps." He held out his hands. "May I offer my assistance in recompense?"

She rested her hands in his, hers long-fingered and white with a few odd nicks on them, his broad and far too brown and callused for a gentleman's hands. Neither of them wore gloves. "You're hands are cold."

She sprang to her feet and tucked her hands behind her back. "I was writing, so took my gloves off—the hateful things. Rowena and Mama will strangle me if I go in there without gloves on. Will you give them my regrets and explain I'll be down in a moment? This birthday party—" She clapped a hand to her mouth, and he noticed an ink stain on the back of her wrist of all places. She started to turn away.

He caught hold of her elbow. "Wait. It's an utter crush in there. Unless there's someone you wish to see"—he glanced at the rosebuds—"why do you not come driving with me?"

"Because Rowena expects me to be here for her at-home."

"Perish the thought of you missing it. All the gentlemen here appear otherwise occupied."

Her nostrils flared. "So I won't be missed?"

"No, of course not."

She winced, then clasped her hands together at her bosom and staggered back a step, fetching up against the banister. "Oh, you wound me to my soul. A direct hit, a—"

"Cut line." He pretended to laugh at her antics, but he knew that wince had been a genuine flinch at his unthinking words. Without realizing he was doing so, he'd invited her for a drive to spare her the humiliation of being the only female in the room with no gentlemen callers. Even Lady Monmouth had a circle of admirers gathered around her settee. No one appeared to await Clarissant's arrival, at least not with any eagerness, just like no one had noticed his arrival, since the butler hadn't bothered to announce him.

"You'll spare me from being one of many in there," he said, trying to make amends for his thoughtlessness.

Would he forever say the wrong thing to this young lady who had once been a body to whom he could say anything without her caring? She had changed so much to now expect even him to pay court to her.

Except she'd run off even when he told her she was beautiful.

Of all things, telling Clarie she was beautiful. Yet she had been in her ball gown and tumbled hair.

A band of sunlight squeezed through a narrow window to light her face, and he realized she was still beautiful. She didn't possess Rowena's classic perfection. She boasted something far stronger.

Character?

He gave himself a mental shake for such a disloyal thought, and an outward shrug for Clarissant's benefit. "No doubt you're awaiting someone to call for you." He glanced at the rosebuds that kept drawing his gaze.

She rubbed at the ink stain on her wrist. "No one in particular. A drive would be nice. I'll fetch my things." With a graceful dignity he didn't know she possessed, she headed up the steps.

Tristan retrieved his hat and driving gloves from the hall table and started down to the ground floor to instruct a footman to have his phaeton returned. Behind him, he heard Rowena's voice raised in a trill of laughter. It sounded light and as pretty as ever, but perhaps a trifle thin, as though she'd employed it so often to charm, she was wearing it out.

Whatever possessed him to have such an uncharitable thought about Rowena? That she'd married to spare her family from poverty rather than preserving her own happiness raised her in his esteem. She was selfless and kind besides being beautiful. He might stop loving her in time, but loving another would still feel like treachery to a lady like her.

So why had he asked Clarie to drive with him?

Tooling along Rotten Row with Clarie tucked beside him, regaling him with tales of her brother Dunstan's antics, Tristan knew why. No one ever made him laugh like Clarie always had.

He grasped his side with one hand. "I don't think I've laughed so hard since I left England."

Her face sobered beneath the brim of her chip straw hat with its fluttering lavender ribbons. "I suppose you didn't have much to laugh about in the Army."

"I didn't have much to laugh about after the Army either."

"And when was that?"

"I officially resigned my commission once I reached India." He hesitated to choose his words carefully. "That was the first British outpost I came across after that merchantman rescued me."

"Did it take a great deal of time to sail to India?"

"Three and a half—" He stopped himself barely in time. "We took three and a half months just to reach the West Indies. Storms. Dodging privateers." He shrugged. "I lost track of time. I liked being at sea. There's a ship leaving for America in a week. I think I'll take a berth on that."

"Good."

"What?" Tristan reined in his team and turned to stare at her. "Did you say good?"

She tilted her head sideways so her brim shadowed her face. "Of course I did. You were obviously happier at sea than you are here, so it's good for you to return to it."

"Well, yes, of course it is."

Then why didn't it feel like it was? Because he'd expected Clarissant to object to him leaving so soon?

Balderdash. She wouldn't miss him much more than she missed Dunstan. Probably less. She hadn't seemed all that excited to see him again after all this time.

Except she'd sniped about him not talking to her since their arrival in London. Clever minx. Perplexing female. Beautiful lady. How could little Clarie have turned into all three?

Not Clarie—Clarissant. She was no child now deserving a child's diminutive name. She was a young lady of quality, looks, charm—when she chose to employ it—a sharp tongue, a sharper wit, and an intensity about her that made him nervous.

Yes, nervous. He'd faced down French pirates without more than a twinge of apprehension, but the sight of Clarissant Behn in her lavender gown and those dratted rosebuds caused him to want to set her down and drive off.

Just as she had run off on him the night before after he told her she was beautiful.

What ridiculous thoughts he was having. In the past, he wanted only to alternatively laugh at or shake Clarie. But Clarissant . . .

He turned his head so he couldn't even see her from

the corner of his eye—and saw a gentleman bow from astride a skinny hired hack. Bow to whom? Clarissant? Tristan couldn't see her response, but when the man straightened, his gaze met Tristan's. The contact lasted no more than a heartbeat, but he experienced the odd sensation that he knew the haggard-looking stranger.

"Who is he?" Clarissant asked.

Tristan twisted in his seat to catch another glimpse of the shabbily dressed man, but he had disappeared beyond a phalanx of carriages. "I don't know him."

"He looked like he knew you," Clarissant said.

"He looked like he was bowing to you." Tristan nudged her with his elbow. "Your secret admirer?"

"If my admirer is secret, how can I know?" She sounded so prim, Tristan laughed.

"Touche." Tristan concentrated on guiding his team out of the park and onto Hyde Park Corner. Traffic was heavy at that time of the afternoon with most of the *haut ton* descending on the park to see and be seen and enjoy flirtations between carriages. He thought he caught a glimpse of Rowena in the distance. When they drew abreast of the carriage, he realized that her companion was her husband.

She gave him a surprised lift of her eyebrows. "So that's where Clarie disappeared. You naughty girl, Clarie, running off. Sir Henry Deville was looking for you."

"Who," Clarissant asked through her teeth, "is Sir Henry Deville?"

Rowena shrugged. "I have no idea. He seemed respectable, though, if somewhat shabby, and he had letters of introduction. I thought you knew him, and was sooo pleased *someone* wanted to call on you." She twirled her white parasol. "He said something about the opera tonight."

Clarissant emitted a noise like a feline growl low in her throat.

Seasham cast his wife a stern glance. "We're holding up traffic here. Good day, Clarissant, Apking. Shall we see you at the opera tonight?"

Tristan almost said no, since he preferred more plebian music, but changed his mind. "Yes, sir, I'll be there."

Clarissant started beside him as they drove off. "You're coming to the opera?"

He shrugged. "I don't see why not."

"I thought you were avoiding Rowena."

He jerked the reins and nearly sent the horses down someone's area steps. "Don't be absurd, child. I've . . . um . . . been occupied."

"Of course you have." She didn't sound convinced.

Why should she? She was right, and, if he was going to, if not outright lie about the past six years, at least not talk about it. At least he could be honest with her about one thing. Perhaps that would make him more comfortable around her. He didn't like not being comfortable with Clarissant, the one person in the world he remembered never feeling uneasy around—except for every time since his return to England.

He drew up in front of the Seasham townhouse, but didn't get down or offer Clarissant assistance to the ground. "Clarie?" He made himself look directly at her. "Clarissant, as much as I want to, I can't simply stop loving someone because I know she is completely beyond me now. I've loved her all my life, and just because she sacrificed her happiness with me for the sake of her family doesn't change matters of the heart. Can you understand that?"

Her lips compressed and her eyes shielded behind curling lashes, she nodded.

"So if I am not about as much as I was in the past," he continued, "it's not because you aren't important to me. You're like a sister to me, and I miss you when I'm gone. But seeing you means seeing Row, and . . ." Feeling like a fool for saying too much, he finished with a shrug. "One day you'll love someone and understand."

She already knew how it felt.

As she stared down at the invitation list for Thomas' birthday party, Clarissant wondered if Tristan had read the same pain in her eyes that she had witnessed in his. Out of her own hurt, she wanted to lash out, tell him that Rowena was no angel, that she hadn't married to save the family but to save herself from poverty and spinsterhood. But what good would hurting him further do? He didn't love her. Knowing the truth about Rowena wouldn't destroy his lifelong love for her in an instant and turn his heart toward Clarissant. No doubt he would want nothing to do with the Behns.

Clarissant hoped he did sail on that ship. Perhaps she could get over him herself if he left before paying her any more pretty compliments and giving her silly heart hope, or treated her so much like a child she wanted to act like one and do something absurd like drop a snake down his back at the opera.

Despite herself, she grinned at the notion. Ah, where was Dunstan when one needed a twelve-year-old boy?

She could bribe him into some sort of trickery with wildlife. But Dunstan was likely frolicking around the estate, happy that Mossy's absence meant no reading lessons for a few weeks. He had geography and mathematics with the curate, but he liked geography and mathematics.

Had Dunstan had a fifth birthday party? She didn't think so. She didn't recall any child having one at so young an age, and wondered why Seasham would want to drag his small children down to London at the height of the season.

She didn't wonder for long. Seasham was no fool. In his subtle way, he was letting Tristan know that Rowena hadn't waited for him. Rowena objected because she didn't want Tristan to know of her faithlessness. She might not love Tristan, but she didn't want to lose his adulation.

No, that was uncharitable. She didn't want to hurt Tristan any more than she already had. Rowena was self-centered, but she wasn't cruel.

Tristan would spare himself the pain of learning when Rowena married if he went to sea in a week. She would encourage him to go.

Clarissant wished she could join him on that ship. New Orleans seemed like such an exotic place. French. Spanish. English. American. An enormous river.

She'd liked geography, too, and wished that Tristan would talk about his adventures at sea. If they had been unpleasant, Clarissant could understand his reluctance to talk about them. But he wanted to return to his explorations of new locations. So why wouldn't he tell her anything about his six years away from them? What had he done that had brought him such a fortune as he displayed? If he invested in cargoes, she would like to know how to go about it. She'd love to expand her perfume business to exports. Already, she planned to ship a few crates to the English colonies in India. Amidst the alien fragrances of the Far East, English ladies might welcome the scents of England. The possible financial rewards outweighed the risk of losing everything.

If only she could consult with Tristan, he could advise her on the practicalities of exporting to foreign lands and the likelihood of profit. Surely trading was how he'd obtained his wealth. They could make plans . . .

All she had to plan right at that moment was a social event, something she disliked. The expense!

And thinking of expense, her opera cloak had set her back far too much. Somehow, Mama had gotten ahold of the designer and insisted on ermine trim. The dressmaker had been kind enough to Clarissant to keep it at a minimum but she hadn't wanted to offend the lady she thought held the pursestrings.

"I should have let her know who is really paying the bills," Clarissant grumbled to her list of families with small children. "Fur trim indeed."

But once she wore the deep blue satin and white fur creation, even Clarissant admitted it suited her well. The blue in the cloak and gown brought out the fact that her eyes were really blue and seemed to add luster to her hair. Her looks couldn't hold a candle to Gwen's vivid coloring nor Rowena's delicate floral hues, yet she knew she would pass. As a last-minute touch she decided to wear the pink rosebuds. Perhaps an admirer was what she needed.

An admirer who had knocked her down and smelled mildly of mildew? She supposed odder things occurred. Usually not at the opera, though.

Settling into the Seasham box to the side of the stage where everyone could see their party, Clarissant focused her thoughts more on whether or not Tristan would attend than whether or not the sender of the rosebuds would announce himself.

Then the music began, and she needed to concentrate on not clapping her hands to her ears and howling like a dog on Guy Fawke's Day. She liked music—which was why the emaciated blond screeching on stage proved so offensive to her ears. No one else seemed to notice how badly the singers—Clarissant applied the term out of respect for the performers' audacity to go on the stage—executed the drama, for they talked and laughed so loudly they nearly drowned out the music. Gentleman after gentleman crowded into the box to admire and be admired. Even a few ladies arrived to draw the gentlemen's attention from Rowena and Gwen as much as possible.

To Clarissant's surprise, she saw Ian hovering on the edge of the throng, and squeezed her way to his side. "What brings you here?"

He bowed, looking rather dashing. "I like music."

Clarissant laughed. "As I said, what brings you here?"

He grinned, and she realized how very handsome he was when he did so; it softened his craggy features. "It is bad, is it not?" His grin faded, and he glanced to where Gwen sat with one gentleman holding a glass of lemonade for her and another plying her fan. "I thought

I'd like a look at her in her opera finery, and perhaps a wee word or two."

"Oh, Ian." Clarissant laid her hand on his arm. "You know it's no good hoping like this."

"Aye, I ken, but my heart does not."

For the second time, Clarissant wondered if perhaps she should set her cap for him in an attempt to draw his attention away from Gwen—as if she could compete with such a pretty, lively lady. But it might distract him long enough for Gwen to get herself betrothed.

She tugged on his elbow. "Walk with me in the passage. This crush is stifling me."

"If you like." With another glance at Gwen, Ian led Clarissant into the passageway behind the boxes where the air did not reek so badly of overheated and perfumed bodies.

"I shouldn't care that ladies like to dose themselves in scent," Clarissant confided. "It makes me at least comfortably off. But it's an insult to my perfumer's nose."

"Our sales always increase in the summer too. When it overpowers me, I just remind myself 'tis the scent of money." Ian turned at the end of the passage and headed back toward the Seasham box just as a gentleman lifted the curtain and vanished inside.

Clarissant wrinkled her nose, trying to place where she'd seen him before, then turned her attention back to Ian. "Perhaps we can develop scented powders for ladies and gentlemen, too, to apply during the warmer months. Powder would absorb moisture and not be as powerful as perfume oils."

Ian nodded. "I do not ken why not. The hair powders

of the last century were often scented, and ladies use rice powder on their faces."

Clarissant thought aloud as they passed the Seasham box and joined a growing promenade of couples strolling the passageway. "Rose is always popular, but perhaps something more delicate. And sandalwood or even almond for gentle—oh!" She gasped as a hand shot out of nowhere and plucked the rosebuds from her waist sash. Her gaze flashed from hand to sleeve to the face of the flower thief. "Tristan! Give those back."

He shoved them into his coat pocket. "They're wilted."

"Not at all." She reached out, then realized she couldn't snatch them out of his pocket in the corridor behind the opera boxes. The petals were starting to fray around the edges, and they no longer mattered anyway. If the sender were there, he'd likely seen her wearing them already.

Casting a grin her way, Tristan bowed to Ian. "Good evening, McLean. No taste for the music?"

"Nay, sir, not this music."

"And I thought it only my common preference for Welsh ballads." Tristan looked at Clarissant. "And you?"

"I've heard better on street corners. Have you seen your sister?"

Tristan smiled. "I have. She's doing well for herself, is she not? Both of the gentlemen attending on her at present are completely suitable, and she looks so happy."

Beside Clarissant, Ian tensed.

She patted his arm, then drew her hand free. "You

can return to sea without fears for Gwen's future. You can count on me for that."

"And Rowena." Tristan gave a little cough. "Lady Seasham, that is. She seems to be a fine chaperone. Ah, the music has stopped."

Indeed it had. If possible, the volume of the audience increased with the dwindling of the orchestra and vocals, and people began pouring from the boxes. Clarissant and her companions stepped aside to allow the Seasham party to exit for air and refreshments.

Eyes glowing, Gwen paused in the doorway to dart a glance from Ian to Clarissant to her brother, then back to Clarissant. "Where are your roses?"

"Your brother stole them."

"Oh?" She arched perfect eyebrows. "Don't you want Clarie to have admirers?"

"Of course I do, but—good evening, Lady Seasham." Tristan bowed to Rowena, who exited the box with a tall, spare gentleman in tow.

Rowena nodded to Tristan and Ian, then focused her huge blue eyes on Clarissant. "This gentleman wishes me to present you to him. Sir Henry, this is my, ha ha, little sister Clarissant Behn. Clarie, Sir Henry Deville."

"Pleased to meet you, sir." Clarissant held out her gloved hand. As Sir Henry took it in his, stepping closer to her, she couldn't stop her nose from twitching at the unmistakable, however faint, odor of mildew clinging to his clothes as though they'd been put away damp. She also believed he was the man who had bowed to Tristan in the park.

Hastily, not too hastily she hoped, she released his

hand and stepped back. "Allow me to present my friends, Tristan Apking and Ian Mc . . ." Her voice trailed off, for she saw Tristan's and Sir Henry's faces as they stared at one another up close.

Both looked as though they were seeing ghosts.

Chapter Nine

"**I**'m mistaken." Tristan paced the floor of his rooms, while McLeod, his valet, groom, and general man of business attempted to expunge the scent of crushed roses from his coat.

Upon seeing the man introduced as Sir Henry Deville, Tristan had crushed his hand against his pocket where he'd thrust the flowers he'd taken from Clarissant. He'd wanted to destroy those delicate blooms, but not into the fine wool of his coat. The fragrance clung, reminding him of Rowena. He'd always considered rose scent as beautiful and delicate as she was. Not now. It would forever remind him of that moment in the opera house when he faced memories of the most horrifying and yet most rewarding day of his life.

"I have to be mistaken," he continued. "Mac, there is no way in the world an Englishman was aboard that French pirate ship."

"You were aboard a French merchantman for a while," McLeod pointed out.

Tristan glared at him. "I was a prisoner until that English ship saved us."

"Maybe he was a prisoner too." McLeod held the coat to his nose, sniffed, and returned to sponging and airing in front of the fire. "Englishmen could have rescued him too."

"He was fighting that day." Tristan closed his eyes to blot out the memories, saw them more clearly, and snapped his lids up again. "I know he was fighting of his own will."

"And how can you be sure of that, sir?"

Tristan flexed his right hand. "I disarmed him."

McLeod dropped the coat. "You fought him yourself?"

"I did. Then someone knocked me down from behind, and when I recovered, I was back aboard our ship and the rest of them had let the pirates go."

Mcleod grinned. "Aye, they did, sent them off without a farthing of booty."

McLeod had joined their crew later, but he'd known the story because everyone told it so often. The English merchantmen fought off and defeated French pirates. The merchantmen didn't want prisoners or another ship, so they sent the pirate ship and crew on its way with food and water enough for a few days, and nothing else. They took everything of value from the ship. Although he had invested his substantial share in varying enterprises, the backbone of Tristan's fortune came from that day. But he would only discuss that with McLeod. Society didn't like money they might view as unclean or stolen in that way. Not even military officers received prize money for pirate ships or the cargoes they captured. For a merchantman, no one even needed to know what they'd done in the middle of the Indian Ocean in the middle of a war.

A war that made an Englishman aboard a French pirate ship attacking Englishmen a traitor.

Tristan shook his head and paused to move the kettle over the fire. He needed tea. Since his return to England, he couldn't seem to drink enough tea, a commodity scarce aboard ship most of the time unless it was the cargo and therefore untouchable.

"No English traitor would have the audacity to come back and join society," he decided aloud.

McLeod carried the coat to the window, opened the latter to air smelling of coal smoke and the river, and hung the former from the sill. "I'm figuring coal smoke's a sight better to smell than roses. Next time, don't go putting ladies' flowers in your pocket."

"I wouldn't have, except—"

Why had he snatched Clarissant's flowers and stuffed them into his pocket? He thought they looked very pretty with her blue gown. But he didn't like some stranger having sent them to her. He needed to protect her. She was like his sister. She shouldn't be encouraging the attentions of gentlemen who didn't announce their names with gifts.

Nor, he thought grimly, should she encourage the attentions of her family's man of business. They'd looked more than a little cozy walking arm and arm up and down that corridor. But the man was a rake, surely.

Once he'd spoken, Tristan realized he was the man who'd been in the Seasham garden with a young lady the night before. McLean was definitely not good enough for Clarissant.

Neither was Deville. His clothes said he couldn't afford to support a wife with any comfort, and he was a traitor.

Tristan started to protest the notion again, but remembered the shock on Sir Henry's face. Had he recognized him too?

"Should I report Deville to Bow Street?" he asked.

McLeod still hung out the window flapping the coat about. "Never do so, sir. They'd think you had gone round the bend or had a vendetta against him, him being a knight and you a nobody and Welsh at that."

"Sound advice, I have no doubt."

McLeod drew in from the window and eyed the coat with disgust. "It'll never do."

"It'll fade in time." What did he care about one coat when he'd likely be heading back to sea? "If the man is the traitor I think he is, should he get away with it?"

"Nay, sir, but you said it—you think he is. You aren't sure, are you? So how do you convince Bow Street?"

"Probably I'll end up being suspected myself because of the fortune I came home with."

The kettle began to bubble. Tristan poured boiling water over leaves in the waiting pot. Fragrant steam rose to his nose, and he inhaled deeply.

Suddenly, he remembered Clarissant doing that upon meeting Sir Henry Deville. She'd gotten an odd look on her face, too, rather like she'd smelled something unpleasant. Tristan had noticed nothing, but then, he'd been overwhelmed with the notion of crushed roses in his pocket. He'd have to ask her. Of course, that meant risking seeing Rowena again. Perhaps early in the morning Rowena wouldn't be awake yet. She never had been an early riser, whereas Clarissant had never failed to be up with the dawn, picking flowers, washing her face with dew, helping the maids at the home farm milk the cows, picking more flowers.

She'd picked flowers that first day he'd been back to Monmouth Hall. Whatever would a young lady do with all those silly flowers? He never saw them in vases about the house. Yet the gardens extended through what used to be groves of oaks. So many things had changed during his absence. Even Clarissant. Especially Clarissant. Yet she still possessed her good sense. At least he thought she did. She seemed sensible except for setting her cap at a man like McLean—if she had. She might fancy someone else. She'd worn those roses all day, and if Deville sent them, the mystery of the man might attract her.

If that occurred, Tristan would certainly have to question the man's loyalty to England, find out somehow if he were the same man he'd fought aboard that pirate ship.

No, he would warn her against the man now.

But that might lead to telling her about how he'd obtained his fortune.

Clarissant laughed down at Ian as he assisted her from his phaeton. Apparently in high humor that morning, he'd kept her amused all the way from the perfumery with his observations on the opera. They were also pleased that they'd found a trader willing to play middleman for their English scents abroad. He even mentioned America as a possible market, now that their two countries seemed bent on gaining friendly ground and trade relations. Greater trade meant greater profits and a brighter future for her family and Ian, and he'd been more talkative than usual.

Alighting on the pavement before the Seasham townhouse, Clarissant twinkled up at her manager from beneath the brim of her lilac-silk bonnet. "You know, Ian, you shouldn't disparage English opera that way. You know what we say about the pipes."

"Aye, I've heard many an ill comment about the pipes, but most are not repeatable before a lady."

"Then you shouldn't mention them at all."

Clarissant jumped at the new voice and spun toward it. "Tristan, why do you keep sneaking up on a body like this?"

He lounged against the railing by the steps leading down to the service door. "I wasn't sneaking up on anyone. I've been here for a full five minutes. You just didn't notice me."

"Because I don't expect to see a gentleman hanging about the steps." She turned to Ian. "Do you care to come in for a cup of coffee? It's a bit chill today."

"Not too chill for a drive," Tristan murmured.

Clarissant chose to ignore him, not having any notion what was wrong with him. She kept looking at Ian, noting the tightness that had formed around his mouth. "No one will be awake yet."

"Which is why you shouldn't be out with a . . . gentleman," Tristan said.

Still choosing to ignore him, Clarissant headed up the front steps. "Come along. You must be cold."

"Thank you, no." Ian removed his hat, bowed, then turned back to his vehicle. "I need to be about my business."

Tristan passed Clarissant and wrapped the door knocker. "Clever man."

"I'll see you day after tomorrow, then," Clarissant said to Ian. She said nothing to Tristan until after a footman let them into the house, took Tristan's hat and gloves, and assured them he would have coffee and rolls brought into the breakfast parlor. Then she shut the door despite the impropriety of a single lady being alone with a gentleman in a closed room, and planted her hands on her hips. "Explain yourself, sirrah."

Tristan, too much of a gentleman to sit while she stood, wasn't too much of one to lounge against the mantel and shove his hands into his pockets. "There's nothing to explain."

"You behaved abominably to Ian."

"I?" He arched eyebrows as perfectly shaped as his sister's.

Unfair, Clarissant thought, her annoyance with him fueled. She was a female and had to pluck her eyebrows to form that curved line, whereas Tristan, a male, likely cared little about their perfection.

"At least my eyelashes are longer," she muttered.

His eyes widened. "What?"

Her cheeks heated. "Never you mind. I don't like your feigned innocence. You were deliberately rude to

Ian, and why were you skulking about the steps anyhow?"

"I passed you two on the way here. You looked so engrossed, I wanted to know what was about between you."

Was he jealous?

Clarissant's heart leaped. *Foolish heart. Of course he's not jealous.*

Then why care if she drove out with Ian?

"Your brother-in-law is obviously not keeping a proper eye on you," Tristan continued, "so I thought some male relative should look out for your interest, and Ian McLean—"

"You are not a male relative." Clarissant's tumble from hope to reality made her tone sharper than necessary. "We share no blood relationship.

"You're as good as my younger sister."

"You've already got Gwen—"

"And McLean isn't good enough for her either."

"Why? Because he's a Scot, Mister Welshman?"

"Because he can't support you."

"Like you couldn't support Rowena when you tried to elope—" Clarissant clapped a hand across her mouth and took a step backward. "I'm sorry," she said from behind her hand. "I–I should go work on the birthday party."

In one stride, Tristan reached her side and caught hold of her hand. "Don't you dare run away from me."

"I'm not—"

He tugged on her hand, drawing her toward a sofa. "You are. But you're going to stop right now. Sit down and tell me what Ian McLean is to you."

"My—our man of business." Clarissant resisted his attempt to make her sit. The sofa was green, a beautiful color for Rowena, not complimentary at all to Clarissant. "You know that."

"I know you two are friendlier than is the usual situation between a daughter of the family and a man of business." Still holding Clarissant's hand, Tristan sat, compelling her to do the same. "So do you have an interest for him?"

The door opened as he demanded this information, and Gwen skipped into the room, red curls bouncing. "Does she have an interest for who?"

Behind her, Miss Moss grimaced. "For whom, my dear, for whom."

"That's what I want to know," Gwen said.

"No one," Clarissant snapped.

She caught Mossy's disapproving glance and realized she still held Tristan's hand. Or he still held hers.

"Ian McLean," Tristan said.

Clarissant yanked her hand free and started to protest again, then caught sight of Gwen's face. Surely her eyes shone a little less brightly than when she erupted into the parlor. If she still found Ian attractive despite her numerous eligible beaux, Clarissant should do her best to nip that in the bud. And her foolish, foolish heart still hoped that perhaps Tristan would stop thinking of her as Rowena's little sister . . .

Clarissant stood, forcing Tristan to do the same out of courtesy. "Ian and I are good friends, and I like him well. What is wrong in that?"

"You driving out with him this morning," Tristan said.

"She drove out with him this early?" Gwen's voice fairly squeaked.

Mossy gave Clarissant a speculative glance, then smiled. "I'll see to some breakfast." She left the room.

Clarissant removed her gloves and cloak and tossed them onto the pale green sofa. "I'll drive out with whomever I please. There is nothing improper about it."

"You drove out with him yesterday too," Tristan pointed out. "I saw you. And you walked alone with him at the opera."

Clarissant yanked a chair out from the small breakfast table. "And what if I do wish to encourage his attentions? It's not as though I have a string of beaux lined up at the door, and he is a gentleman."

"When he was alone with a young lady in the garden at the ball?" Tristan's voice raised a few decibels.

Gwen paled.

Clarissant smiled. "So were you."

"That was different," Tristan declared.

"Why?" Clarissant and Gwen demanded together.

"Because I was with you, not a young lady."

Clarissant dropped into the chair she held so she didn't hurl it at him.

Gwen gasped. "Tristan Apking, how can you be so rude to Clarissant? Clarie, are you going to let him talk to you that way? Go ahead, tell him what you think of him."

Clarissant couldn't tell him anything. She realized she'd also sat down because her legs were shaking. She didn't trust her voice to work right. She'd either say regrettable things to him, or she would burst into tears.

A footman entered with a tray of coffee and tea at that moment, and she wanted to hug him for his timely arrival. Setting out cups and saucers and pouring hot drinks gave her time to recover her equilibrium. Then Mossy arrived with another footman carrying rolls and coddled eggs. By the time the servants left, Clarissant knew she could speak without stammering or weeping.

"I never knew you considered me less than a lady, Tristan. Or is it that I'm quite aged at three and twenty?"

"Oh, Clarissant." Seated across the table from her, he scrubbed his hands over his face, then shoved his fingers into the thick, dark red hair at his temples as though his head hurt. "You know I didn't mean it that way."

"I don't think she does know that," Gwen said, while lavishly buttering a bread roll. "She looks like she wants to hit you."

"Miss Gwenevere," Mossy reproved.

"How did you mean it?" Gwen asked around a bite of the buttered roll.

Tristan cast Clarissant a beseeching glance. "You do understand me, do you not?"

She did know what he meant, but that was what hurt, so she gave him no help.

He sighed. "I only meant that she's as good as a sister to me."

"She is not anything like a sister to you," Gwen declared. "We aren't even distant cousins."

"We were brought up like siblings," Tristan protested.

"But Rowena was good enough to marry and Clarissant is only a sister?"

Clarissant wondered if she could vanish into thin air

or slide under the table and be forgotten. She glanced to Miss Moss for help, but that dear woman merely gave her a bland gaze in response.

Tristan choked on his tea, and Gwen sat straight and cool like Boudicca surveying the defeated Romans. Clarissant just wished she knew what the victory was.

Tristan closed his eyes, looked as though he was praying, then opened them to fix a baleful glare upon his sister. "Rowena is my age, not—"

"Don't remind her of that."

"And Clarissant is a little . . . er . . . younger . . . er—"

"Well, if you can't see how beautiful she is," Gwen broke in, "you deserve to have her fall for a mere man of business like Mister McLean, or an impoverished baronet like Sir Henry Deville."

Tristan knocked over his tea. Brown liquid streamed across the white tablecloth and straight for Clarissant.

She jumped out of harm's way and tossed her serviette onto the growing stain.

With a groan, Tristan cradled his head in his hands.

"Tristan Apking," Gwen asked in a gentle tone, "are you foxed?"

"Not a bit of it." Slowly, he rose and began rolling up the soiled cloth. "I've had only tea. It's you females—"

"Us females?" Gwen and Clarissant said together.

"You were the one who said Clarie isn't a young lady," Gwen pointed out.

"And badgered me about driving out with Ian," Clarissant added.

Miss Moss seemed to be having a difficult time not

choking on her own tea. Above her compressed lips, her eyes twinkled with amusement.

Tristan sighed. "I only meant that neither Lady Monmouth nor Rowena would object to me walking in the garden with Clarissant because we've known one another so long. She's not like a strange young lady."

"An excellent start, Mr. Apking," Mossy said.

Tristan crushed the tablecloth between his hands. "As to objecting to her driving out with Ian McLean, I think she can do better than her family's man of business."

"So what is your objection to Sir Henry?" Gwen asked.

Tristan glanced at Clarissant, and his eyes held an appeal as he spoke. "I don't yet know of anything, but . . . dash it all, I came over this morning to see if Clarissant would like to go for a drive with me, not argue with anyone."

"It's raining." Mossy rose. "I'll fetch another cover and more tea. Miss Gwenevere, don't you have an appointment with the bootmaker this morning?"

"I forgot." Gwen sprang up. "That's why I'm up so early. I'm determined to learn to ride, and I can't do it without proper boots." She all but sprinted out of the room, Mossy following with more dignity.

Tristan held Clarissant's gaze. "May we have a civil conversation now?"

Her tummy fluttering, Clarissant affected a nonchalant shrug. "I've always been civil."

"No, you—" Tristan grinned. "All right, I was a bit rough on McLean. But I do care about you and want the best for you."

You are the best for me.

But he didn't view it that way. If he ever realized it, he would be long gone to sea and likely never trusting another Behn to wait for him.

As if he ever would realize how well they'd suit.

Clarissant moved to sit on the Pomona-green sofa, even though the yellowish green light made her skin sallow. "So what is your objection to Sir Henry?"

"That's actually what I came to discuss with you." He glanced at the door. "Alone."

"Mossy won't come back for a bit."

Bless her. She likely thought she was doing Clarissant a favor leaving her alone with Tristan. If only . . .

"What's amiss with Sir Henry?" Clarissant asked, though she had her own opinions.

Why would a man smell of mildew? And if he was the man who had knocked her down at the ball, why had he done it, then decided to pay court to her?

Tristan took a turn about the parlor, drawing back the curtain long enough to show Gwen dashing from house to carriage with a footman holding an umbrella over her and one of the maids who would accompany her to Bond Street. Rain made the scene look like they were staring through a waterfall.

Not a good day for shopping, calling, or her excursion to Gunters to choose confections for the party. Good. Clarissant wanted a day at home. And if Tristan remained until the rain let up, perhaps they could retreat to the library where she could remind him of his favorite books that had also been hers, of the way she always beat him at ducks and drakes, of how she wanted to venture out into the world and once lamented that females couldn't take a grand tour or join the Army.

Tristan faced her, his hands fisted against his thighs. "Clarissant, I have no way to prove this, and I'm not completely certain, but I believe Sir Henry Deville is a traitor to England."

Chapter Ten

"A traitor?" Clarissant squeaked the words just as her mother sailed through the doorway on a cloud of heliotrope—not one of Clarissant's scents.

"Did I hear you say you'd sent for a tray?" she asked.

Clarissant exchanged a glance of amusement with Tristan and nodded. "Mossy is seeing to it, Mama. Do say good morning to our caller."

"Oh, Tristan, I didn't notice you." Mama gazed myopically at Tristan. "Isn't it a bit early for a call?"

Tristan bowed. "Not when my sister has already departed, ma'am."

"Well," Lady Monmouth said, "you won't see Rowena this early."

Clarissant ground her teeth. "He didn't come to see Rowena, Mama. He came to see Gwen and me."

"Oh." Mama sank onto the chair Tristan pulled out for her. "Why would he come to see you when you're sitting on that sofa? It looks perfectly ghastly behind you."

130

Clarissant jumped up. "Then I'd better move, had I not? I wouldn't want the sofa to look ghastly on my account."

Tristan snorted.

Lady Monmouth looked blank. "You didn't make the sofa ghastly, my dear. It looks perfectly all right now. Ah, here is Miss Moss."

To Clarissant's relief, she saw her companion and friend entering the parlor with another tea tray. Of course, now she and Tristan couldn't discuss Sir Henry any longer, but he didn't seem inclined to leave either.

Miss Moss set the tray on the table. "I'll pour out for your mother, Miss Clarissant. You run along and show Mr. Apking those books he was interested in borrowing."

Clarissant felt her eyebrows shoot up her forehead. Was Mossy playing matchmaker?

Behind Lady Monmouth's chair, she saw Tristan mouth, "What books?"

She smiled. "That's marvelous, Mossy. Tris, take your tea and come up to the library with me."

Nodding, apparently having caught on, Tristan took the two cups Mossy poured, and followed Clarissant up the stairs to the library, a room the Seashams never used except for the gentlemen after-dinner parties. It smelled of cheroots, port and leather, but a fire burned in the grate to keep damp from the fine volumes few people read, lending the room a coziness that invited camaraderie and conversation in two comfortable red brocade chairs pulled up before the fire.

Clarissant seated herself and accepted the cup of coffee Tristan held out to her. "No one will disturb us here."

Though he sat, his teacup balanced on his knee, Tristan looked tight-lipped and disinclined to talk. Worse than disinclined, he looked stormy, his eyes the gray of the sky.

Clarissant set her cup on the hearth. "What's amiss? Would you rather not tell me about Sir Henry?"

"No, I don't want to tell you, but I must." He sipped tea. "But right now, I'm biting my tongue."

"Oh?" Clarissant widened her eyes at him. "Whatever for?"

He set his cup on the hearth hard enough to have likely cracked the china. "Does it not bother you that your mother just insulted you?"

"Not any more." Beneath her breath, she added, "Much."

Why did it bother him?

Her foolish heart was leaping about again. What did it think it was, an Irish jig-monger?

Tristan's fist clenched on the knee of his fawn pantaloons. "You do seem to go along with it. You always did, and I don't like it."

"Why ever not? I am the ugly duckling in the family. No, I'm more like an ugly—"

"Stop it, Clarissant Behn." Tristan seized her hand. "You're a very pretty . . . lady. Excessively pretty. You might not have been six years ago, but now . . . very pretty." His gaze locked with hers.

She couldn't breathe. Her heart had turned into an acrobat. She could have gazed into his clear gray eyes all day.

He broke the contact. His cheeks a tinge darker than normal, he bent forward to retrieve his cup. The saucer was cracked, and he blushed. "I'm so sorry."

Clarissant swallowed, managed to catch her breath and return to normal—on the outside. "No matter. It's not the good china." She licked her dry lips. "Do you wish to warn me against Sir Henry now?"

"Yes. Yes, I must, though you may think the less of me for it."

Now her heart skipped a few beats for a reason other than the hope of her affections being returned. "You aren't . . . you didn't . . ." No, she couldn't think it, let alone say it.

He offered her a half-smile. "No, Clarissant, I'm not a traitor. But I was sailing in the Indian Ocean catching pirates while other Englishmen were fighting the French and Americans."

Clarissant blinked, confused. "You said you were on an English merchantman that rescued you."

"I was. That is, we did trade—the goods we captured."

To give herself a moment to assimilate this, Clarissant retrieved her coffee and retreated behind the cup. "Why don't you start from the beginning?"

"I can." Tristan held his teacup as though warming his hands, though it had to be less than warm now. He looked at the fire, not her. "My troop transport ship went down in the Bay of Biscay. It's famous for storms, and we ran into a bad one with too many inexperienced sailors aboard. The ship broke up. We got as many aboard longboats and onto makeshift rafts as we could, but it didn't matter in the end. The French were waiting for us in the morning, and picked us up like fish in a barrel."

Clarissant shuddered to think of him a prisoner. "But if you were captured, why did we hear you were killed?"

"Bad luck." Tristan shrugged. "Really bad luck when you consider Rowena might have waited for me—" He snapped his teeth together as though biting off the words.

Clarissant gritted her teeth together.

He shook his head. "No help for that now. I think no word got through because an English privateer merchantman captured the French corvette I was on and freed us English if we agreed to come with them. Of course I did. We all did. I thought they'd get me back to Portsmouth and I could report for duty, perhaps even pay a visit to your family. But they were sailing for the Far East. I didn't see an English Army post for two and a half years."

"But"—Clarissant shook her head to clear it—"the war was over by then."

Tristan inclined his head, but said nothing. Silence fell over the room save for the patter of rain against the windows and the occasional rumble of a carriage trundling by in the square. No one seemed to stir in the house, for it was quiet even with the door half open for the sake of propriety.

Unable to bear the stillness another moment, Clarissant dove headfirst into what could be deep water indeed. "Did you have a choice?"

"I don't know." Tristan met her gaze. "That's the dratted thing about it. I don't know if I could have gotten away long enough to report to an English military post or not. They didn't seem inclined to let us. The captain liked having all of us aboard because we won more prizes that way. No one else got away either. But I was an officer. Only a lowly lieutenant to be sure, but still, I was an officer."

He looked so guilty, Clarissant sought for words to reassure him, comfort him. "But you were fighting England's enemies, were you not?"

"I was, and—if you'll forgive the vulgarity—making a great deal of money at it. We made so much off of French pirates that we decided to call in at Calcutta to sell our goods and do some honest trading. That's when the captain let most of the men go, and I had enough money to sell my commission."

"So the military saw nothing wrong in what you were doing?"

"Well, no."

"Then why should you?"

Tristan sighed. "Because I should have tried harder to get home."

"Why didn't you?"

"I wanted to make a fortune by honest means, without the stink of pirate plunder on it. But that never seemed to be enough . . . for her."

Clarissant hesitated a moment, then decided to be bold regardless of the consequences. "Or perhaps you were afraid you didn't love her as much as you did in your dreams?"

"Never." He sounded fierce. "Everything I sacrificed was for her." His shoulders seemed to sag. "But perhaps she needed me instead of gold."

Clarissant resisted the urge to snort at that one. "Tristan." She reached out to him, but didn't have the audacity to take his hand. "Rowena was already married by then. It wouldn't have made any difference when you came home after that."

"I know." He pressed her hand. "But I've been telling people who have the poor taste to ask, that I made my fortune in trade, when in truth I made it in taking cargoes from French ships."

"Cargoes they stole from Englishmen," Clarissant said.

Her conscience pricked her. She deceived everyone about the origin of the Behns' newfound prosperity. Was that wrong? She protected her sister in doing so, for everyone believed Rowena married to help the family and thought her honorable. Clarissant did it so her mother wouldn't worry about anything but what to wear to her next gathering of friends, and Dunstan would have an estate to which he could bring home a wife and on which he could raise his children without the concerns of poverty with which she had grown up. She did it so she could have a purpose in life other than loving a man who would never care for her beyond an affectionate friendship.

So he had helped rid the seas of French pirates to give himself security, and to give security to a lady who hadn't waited for him longer than three months.

She heard Rowena awake now, talking to someone on the floor above. Wanting to distract Tristan, she grabbed the first question that popped into her head. "Why didn't you come home once you got matters straight with the military?"

He glanced toward the doorway where Rowena and Seasham walked past. Neither glanced into the library, for they seemed engaged in a heated discussion.

"Of course she'll do a fine job of planning the party," Rowena was saying.

"But she has little experience planning social events," Seasham protested. "I want everything . . ."

Their voices drifted down the stairs.

Clarissant grimaced. "I'm the topic of discussion with them this morning. Seasham is right. I have little experience, but I'm good at managing things, so it'll be a fine party. Would you like to come to Gunters with Gwen and me this afternoon to choose cakes and ices?"

She'd go despite the rain if he decided to come along.

Tristan shook his head. "Not that I wouldn't enjoy the company, but I've promised the captain of the ship I might sail on that I'd go over cargo inventories with him. He thinks his last supercargo was dishonest."

"Might sail on?" Clarissant seized the phrase with a mixture of hope and apprehension.

If he didn't go, he would be there for the party and learn the painful truth about Rowena. If he did sail, Clarissant might never see him again. She certainly would have no future with him.

As though I have a chance of one with you now.

He shrugged. "That's one reason why I agreed to work with the captain. I want to make certain we deal well with one another before I commit myself to years of working with him. If he's the sort who keeps his crew virtual prisoners, I won't work with him."

"I should think you wouldn't have to work at all." She sounded prim.

"I don't, but I want to."

"Then buy your own ship."

He stared at her. "That could take months."

"Are we so unwelcoming you want to leave us as soon as possible?" She studied his face, needing an honest answer from him.

He remained quiet for a moment, then, looking a little surprised, shook his head. "I was running away from the hurt—" He rubbed at his knee. "I'd never tell anyone else that, Clarie—Clarissant. All I could think for the first fortnight I was here was to get away. Now . . ." He smiled. "I should stay and see Gwen safely betrothed at the least, and keep rakes away from you."

"Like Sir Henry."

He nodded. "Yes, we have rather gotten away from him, have we not?" He drummed his fingers on his knee and gazed into the fire. "I'm probably mistaken. The more I think on it, the more certain I am. The last time I saw him was in the heat of battle. He came at me with a sword and I disarmed him. Wounded him. I got hit on the head after that, so don't have much memory of anything else, so you see why I can't go about maligning the man."

"I do, but . . ." Clarissant's head was reeling. "You're saying you fought Sir Henry Deville aboard an enemy ship? A French pirate ship during the war?"

"If it is he, yes."

"And the if is the difficulty?"

Tristan nodded, then rose to shovel more coal onto the fire. "If I'm wrong, I could ruin the man."

"But what if you're not wrong?"

Gwen licked a dainty morsel of strawberry ice off her spoon, and nodded in approval. "Any five-year-old who doesn't like a pink ice is destined for Newgate, they would be that odd."

Clarissant glanced around the confectioner's shop, sparse with patrons on the third rainy afternoon in a row and her third and final attempt to reach Gunters. Those patrons present drank hot chocolate and nibbled at dainty cakes that would never suit small children. "I don't like pink ices."

"But you're not five."

"I didn't when I was five. I much prefer lemon and—ugh." She hadn't noticed the candied violet atop a sponge cake before she took a bite of it.

"I'll eat it." Gwen snatched up the confection.

Clarissant shuddered. "How can you bear to eat flowers?"

"Delicious. Any more? Shall we order three dozen of those?"

"No."

What a waste of perfectly good flowers, petrifying them in sugar. The idea made Clarissant's skin crawl.

"I don't think children like them," she said.

"I liked them as children." Gwen selected another cake topped with candied rose petals. "Rowena should like them with the rose scent she wears."

"You're right. I'll order some for the parents. And violets too."

"And pink ices."

"Strawberry and lemon ices." Clarissant drew a pencil and scrap of paper from her reticule and began to write an order. She preferred not to use ink in public for fear of staining her fingers or gown. "Let us see . . .

only five children, since scarcely anyone has theirs in town, but everyone invited will come to honor the little viscount, strange as this party is."

Gwen jabbed her spoon into her ice. "I wish this weren't going to happen at all. You know Tristan will find out how old his little lordship is, and he'll know she didn't even wait for him to leave England. It'll break his heart."

Clarissant took care dotting her letters. "His heart has already been broken."

"I know, and I so want him to fall head over ears for you."

Clarissant made herself laugh. "What a ridiculous thing to say. He thinks of me as a sister."

"I don't know, Clarie. Would someone who is only a brother be so against you flirting with Ian McLean or Sir Henry."

"I was not flirting with them," Clarissant protested a little too vehemently.

She drew the attention of two elderly ladies with spectacles perched upon their noses and hats like bird nests upon their heads.

She smiled at them, then turned back to Gwen. "You know I wasn't flirting with them."

"Yes, I know, but Tris complained about it for ten minutes but didn't say a word about my beaux. Isn't Mister Haley quite the handsomest man you've ever seen?"

He wasn't as handsome as Tristan.

"Do you like him the best?" Clarissant asked.

Gwen took an enormous bite of strawberry ice and

shook her head. When she swallowed, her face grew sad. "I guess I'm like my brother—destined to love someone who has affections elsewhere."

"You're absurd. Whomever could you like who wouldn't adore you in return?"

Gwen snatched the plate from in front of Clarissant. "You're destroying the macaroons. I'm only funning with you. I've decided to marry for position and money instead of love. Love only gets people hurt."

Perhaps she was right. That relieved Clarissant's mind about Gwen having an affection for Ian. She could never marry him if she wanted position and money.

Yet how could dear Gwen not want love for or from her husband?

"I mean, look what Tristan has suffered," Gwen continued. "And even if he's fallen in love with you instead—"

"He hasn't."

"He will still be hurt when he learns that Rowena married three months after she was going to elope with him."

"He won't learn. He's sailing on Tuesday."

Gwen looked puzzled. "No, he's not. Didn't he tell you?"

Clarissant toyed with a ginger biscuit. "No, he didn't. I've scarce seen him since Thursday."

Gwen made a face. "You've been too occupied with Mister McLean, or do you think I don't know about him coming to call?"

Of course Gwen knew. Clarissant wanted her to. Sir Henry hadn't made an appearance, since Rowena didn't have another At Home until that afternoon, but he had sent another bunch of flowers—lilies of the valley this time. They were too sweet for Clarissant, so she gave them to her mother whom they suited much better.

Clarissant feigned embarrassment. "He's shy."

"And so charming with that smile of his." Gwen sounded a bit wistful, and she looked at the rain-drenched window for a moment. Then she flashed Clarissant a mischievous grin. "I made certain Tristan knew when and just how long Mister McLean stayed so he would be jealous."

"But he wasn't, apparently, since he hasn't been to call on me."

"That's because he's gone to Bristol. To look at ships to buy."

"Goodness, he took me seriously?" Clarissant nearly choked on her hot chocolate. "Well, that's wonderful for him."

"It's wonderful for all of us. He'll be back in time for the birthday party and our first night at Almack's. You do know that our vouchers came through, do you not?"

Clarissant sighed. "Yes. Wednesday nights of stale cake and weak punch just to be on display."

"Both my brothers expect me to find a husband this season. I wouldn't wish to disappoint them."

"And Rowena expects it of me." Clarissant wrote cream cakes on the bottom of her list and beckoned for the proprietor to come take her order, then she gathered up her gloves, reticule and cloak. Their maid and a footman appeared from the corner where they'd been enjoying a rare treat of hot chocolate and cakes, and whistled up the carriage. Now she had to wonder how to keep Tristan from coming to the birthday party. Tell him no adults allowed? No, he'd learn the truth. Tell him flat out he wasn't welcome? No, that wouldn't do. Of course he was welcome. Suggest that—

"Oh!" A tug on her wrist yanked the exclamation from her. The footman with the umbrella shouted, and she glanced down to see a small child darting off across the street with her reticule dangling from his hand, the strings cut.

"Catch him. Catch him," Gwen and the maid shrieked together.

The footman started to toss down the umbrella.

"No, don't." Clarissant caught his arm. "I'll be soaked on the way to the carriage, and I paid more for this gown than I carry in my reticule."

"But, Clarie," Gwen protested, "your things you carry."

Clarissant started to shrug off the matter of a comb, pencil, handkerchief, and a few shillings. Then she remembered that she'd made some notes for Ian on one of her scraps of paper. Likely that urchin couldn't read, but if it reached the wrong hands by happenstance, anyone looking through the contents would learn that she knew more about Madame de Fleur's floral essences than a mere society miss should.

Chapter Eleven

At a knock on the library door, Clarissant looked up from her favorite Miss Austen novel with a measure of impatience. After three weeks of a hectic London schedule and a week of preparation before that, she had looked forward to Sunday evening with no balls or soirées to attend. Society didn't stop because of Sunday, but even Rowena would not attend any functions on Sundays. Besides, she and Seasham were entertaining a few friends in the large drawing room, Mama was visiting friends of hers in Berkeley Square, and Gwen was embroidering in her bedchamber. So Clarissant retreated to the library and the pages of *Emma*, and the interruption was not welcome.

"Yes." She knew the single word held considerable impatience.

A maid pushed the door open and peeked around the edge, barely more than her mobcap and eyes showing. "Miss Behn, I know we wasn't to disturb you, but there's a boy in the kitchens insisting he sees you. Cook tried to send him away, but he won't go, and we don't wish to call the watch on a child." Speech delivered, the girl hung her head as though exhausted.

Baffled, Clarissant set her book aside and rose. "Of course you shouldn't call the watch on a child. But whatever can he want?"

The maid retreated from the doorway. "We don't know, Miss. He won't say. He just insists he has a message for you."

"A message?" Alarms shot through Clarissant.

Was something wrong with the perfumery? It wasn't open on Sunday, but still . . .

She hastened to the backstairs, the maid following. "You should have said a message straight away."

"Begging your pardon, Miss." The maid sounded anxious. "We're all at sixes and sevens about it."

"Of course you are." Clarissant softened her tone as she headed down to the kitchen. "You did the right thing." She reached the lower passageway and pushed open the door to the kitchen. Steamy warmth smelling of roast beef, lemon custard, and an unwashed person met her.

So did the eyes of half a dozen servants gathered around the scrubbed pine table in the center of the room, and the hooded gaze of a child huddled beside the fire.

He looked to be perhaps seven or eight, though that was difficult to tell with the grime that covered his face. She judged merely from his size, which was small inside layers of ragged clothing. Long hair hung in tangles down his back, and, when he stood and raised stunningly long lashes to look straight into her face, Clarissant realized that he was really a she.

"We couldn't get rid of him," the butler said. "I can still call the—"

Clarissant held up a silencing hand and addressed the child. "What's your name, girl?"

The clear green eyes widened even further. "How did you—I ain't a girl."

"Of course you are." Clarissant crouched to her level. "What's your name?"

"Don't have one."

"Well, I do. It's Clarissant Behn, and you've come to see me."

Behind her, the servants began to murmur.

Clarissant shook her head at them and continued to focus on the child. "Would you like to give me the message first, or would you like some supper?"

"Don't need no supper." The girl stuck out her chin. "The man who wants the message give to you gave me a meat pie."

A thoughtful man, knowing that coin would be more likely to go to the hands of a parent or someone unscrupulous. Not the sort one would expect to send secret messages by way of street urchins. A matter of concern, but not alarming.

"Good." Clarissant held out her hand. "May I have my message then?"

The girl gnawed her lower lip. "You won't call the watch on me? The man said you wouldn't."

"He's probably right." Clarissant kept her tone even, though she didn't know if she liked the sound of this man who sent messages with a ragged child, yet knew her well enough to figure she wouldn't call the watch on her. "But have you done something wrong?"

The girl hung her head. "Yes, ma'am. I stole your reticule." The little head popped up again. "But I bringed it back." From inside her rags, she withdrew Clarissant's now bedraggled reticule with, judging from its plumpness, the contents still inside.

The servants gasped and began to rise.

The child dropped the article as though it had grown hot, and backed toward the door. "I were wrong to steal it, but I were hungry and—"

"I am fetching the watch," the butler insisted. "And Lord Seasham. This is an outrage."

"That children are stealing because they're hungry, yes." Clarissant picked up her reticule. Hearing the chink of coins, she realized that it still held her few shillings too. "Did you take anything out of it?" she asked the child.

The girl shook her head. "I didn't get no chance. That man paid me t' take it, then snatched it from me soon as I got away."

Grumbles rose from the servants.

Clarissant flashed a withering glance at them, and they fell silent. Then she turned back to the urchin. "Do you work for one of those men who makes children steal for him?"

"No, ma'am." She grabbed the door handle, but the bar was in place, so she wouldn't get far. "I never steal nothin'. I sweep the crosswalks." She'd taken that reticule fast enough for someone who'd never done it before.

Clarissant suppressed a smile for the girl's audacity.

"Then why did you steal my reticule?"

She tugged on the handle. When the door wouldn't budge, she gave it a panicked look, then sagged against it, apparently working out that everyone in the room could catch her before she removed the heavy bar. "T' gentleman paid me to take it."

"What?" Clarissant's own gasp joined those of the watching servants. She gritted her teeth. "Why?"

The girl slumped further. " 'Cause I tried to take his handkerchief. It weren't very good, but my nose were running and I seen the fine ladies . . ." A track of clean skin appeared in the dirt on her face in the wake of a half dozen tears. "My clothes is too dirty."

They were indeed. Clarissant's nose had long since closed up against the stink. Her heart squeezed at the child's plight.

"So did he offer to forget you tried to take his handkerchief in exchange for you stealing my purse?" she asked.

The girl nodded.

The servants snorted in derision, and the butler made more noises of fetching the watch.

The girl nodded. "I was scared he'd send me to Newgate."

And if she hadn't gotten away, would the man have abandoned her to whatever punishment was due her? Or did he count on Clarissant's good graces to keep the child from harm?

Clarissant's good graces.

Finally, the notion that he'd sent the child to steal her reticule and not someone else's sank through her thick skull, and she shot out a hand to grasp the girl's fragile wrist. "Who?"

"Dunno."

"Describe him."

"I can't. It were too rainy and dark and he had an umbrella over his face like. 'Tis why I thought he wouldn't notice me." She dropped to her knees. "But he did, and now you're gonna put me in jail."

"No, child." Clarissant held her outrage in check enough to keep her tone even. "I'll put you in a bath, but not Newgate."

"A bath?" The girl stared at her. "With hot water and everything?"

"And she'll steal the silver," Cook muttered.

"I won't," the girl cried.

"We'll get her cleaned up and send her down to Monmouth," Clarissant said, rising. "See it's done," she addressed the housekeeper. "What's your name, child?"

"Susan, ma'am. Ma called me Susan before she went away."

"Then, Susan, I'll see you're taken care of, but if you take so much as a bun without asking first, you're out the door, all right?"

Susan put her hands together as though pledging an oath of fealty. "I promise, ma'am."

The servants protested, and the butler said he would speak to Lord Seasham. But Clarissant stood firm on helping the child, and was determined to find out why she'd been used.

With Susan in the capable hands of two housemaids who hadn't started out much better off, Clarissant carried her reticule back to the library where she was assured privacy, and dumped the contents onto her lap. Five shillings, a comb, a linen handkerchief and a scrap of paper fell out of the bag. It wasn't the scrap of paper with notes about the perfumery on it. That was missing. This paper was a note.

If you want him to live, tell Tristan Apking to leave England.

Clarissant straightened at the welcome sight of Tristan entering the Almack's Assembly Rooms on Wednesday night. He hadn't returned from Bristol the day before, and now, at ten minutes of eleven o'clock, he risked not being allowed to enter the ball at all. She caught his eye over the heads of the dancers, and he smiled with a warmth that sent her silly heart pounding.

He wouldn't smile for long after she told him about the note.

"Clarissant." Her diminutive mother tugged on her arm.

She bent to hear what her parent wanted to say. "Yes?"

"Don't stand up so straight. Do you want to be a wallflower all evening?"

Dutifully, Clarissant slumped. She really didn't want to be a wallflower. She'd been given permission to waltz and hoped someone would ask her. Someone like Tristan. Ian would have waltzed with her. He'd confided once that he had learned it years earlier and enjoyed the graceful dance. But Ian would never be given admission to such an august assembly as Almack's, where the *creme de la creme* were assured that any future mate they picked was of the finest stock.

Like being a horse at Tattersalls auction.

Clarissant felt rather like a draft horse amidst a stable of Arabians. But she enjoyed watching the pretty sight of others swirling about the floor in their best gowns and evening dress.

Gwen seemed to be spending almost too much time with a young viscount, but she left him on the edge of the dance floor and rushed to greet her brother. They talked for a few minutes, their gazes flashing to Clarissant more than once, then Tristan tweaked Gwen's cheek and skirted the room to make his bow to the patronesses present. Mrs. Drummond-Burrell barely acknowledged his presence, he being a lowly Welshman even though he was the son and brother of a baron, but kind Lady Sefton spent several minutes talking with him.

"You should go fetch some lemonade for me," Mama said. "Then you will look occupied and kindly instead of left out."

With Tristan now heading her way, Clarissant didn't feel in the least left out.

Quite properly, he greeted her mother first, then straightened from his bow to give Clarissant a smile of genuine warmth. "I'm so pleased to see a friendly face. Missus Drummond-Burrell all but gave me the cut direct."

"I think she'd treat Prinney himself that way." Fiddling with her reticule in which she had secured the note, she couldn't offer him a smile in return. "But Lady Sefton spoke with you for a while."

"You noticed?"

Of course she'd noticed.

"She offered to present me to any lady I wished to meet."

"High praise indeed," Mama said. "And you a younger son without a title."

"Just impeccable tailoring," Clarissant murmured. "How did you get such fine evening wear so quickly?"

"Clarissant," Mama scolded, "that's indelicate."

Tristan winked at Clarissant. "Never you mind, Lady Monmouth. We're such old friends, she can ask me anything."

"Clarie's not that old," Mama protested. "She just keeps getting taller, rather like a tree."

"An oak, I suppose," Clarissant said through her teeth.

Tristan compressed his lips, while his eyes danced.

"I was about to fetch Mama and myself some lemonade," Clarissant said. "Will you join me?"

"Clarissant, will you never learn not to be so bold?" Mama sounded shocked. "You never invite a gentleman to go anywhere with you, even if you are friends."

"I do," Clarissant said. She wondered how one pleaded with one's eyes and hoped the glance she shot Tristan was successful at conveying some kind of message of desperation.

He nodded, giving her hope that he did understand her need to escape, then took her hand and tucked it into the crook of his arm. "I would love to join Clarissant for some lemonade, if you do not object, my lady." Without waiting for Lady Monmouth's objection or consent, he turned and led Clarissant toward the refreshment rooms. "Before you explode like a–a—"

"An oak with a charge of gunpowder in a lightning storm?" Clarissant suggested sweetly.

Tristan laughed. "Something of the sort." He paused before entering the refreshment rooms. "You are a bit of an oak, strong and unflappable and—"

"Quiet, or you'll discover that I am not unflappable. I

must talk—drat." The dance ended and couples swarmed toward the refreshments, poor as they were. Soon, scores of people stood, milled or passed too close to them for her to say one word about the note. Yet she dared not wait any longer.

She took a chance at embarrassing herself and getting evicted from Almack's for unseemly behavior and leaned toward Tristan to whisper in his ear. "I need to talk to you."

He gave her an odd look, as well he might. "I'll call on you tomorrow."

She pressed her fingers into his forearm. "No, tonight. Before you leave here."

"Whatever—" He drew his arm from beneath her hand. "Good evening, Rowena."

She dropped him a curtsy. "Good evening, Tristan. I'm so pleased you arrived safely back to London. Will you come to our little party tomorrow? There won't be too many children there to be annoying."

The children, Clarissant thought uncharitably, would not be the annoying members of the party.

"Tristan has business to occupy him," Clarissant said.

He frowned at her. "It can wait. If you wish me there, I will be there."

"Of course we wish for you to be there." Rowena smiled at Clarissant. "Do we not? And Thomas is so adorable at four." Her narrowed gaze warned Clarissant not to give away the lie.

Rowena already knew she wouldn't. Why should she willfully hurt Tristan's feelings, wound his heart any further, by letting him know that Thomas, Viscount Ripon, was really turning five?

Taking Tristan's arm again, Clarissant cast her sister a sugary smile. "Tristan will be bored to tears by the music we have planned. Shall we fetch that lemonade, Tris?"

"Um, yes." Tristan seemed to straighten, then nodded to Rowena and headed for the nearest refreshment table. "Now tell me what's amiss. No, wait, not here. I see Gwen coming. I suppose I'll have to waltz with you."

Clarissant dropped him a deep curtsy. "Thank you for the honor, kind sir. I am so distressed to disappoint you, but I am not yet permitted to waltz."

She didn't know why she lied to him, except that she still stung over the way he'd dropped her hand as soon as Rowena arrived, and now his reluctance to waltz with her reappeared. He couldn't be seen being friendly with her in front of Rowena? All right then, she would send him about his business.

But the note!

He chucked her under the chin. "Minx. Of course you're permitted. I already asked Lady Sefton."

"You . . . you . . ."

"Hush. Spluttering is unbecoming."

Gwen spared Clarissant from having to say anything, since she couldn't think of a word to say she was so surprised. Brother and sister exchanged some lively banter, then Gwen's next partner claimed her, and Tristan led Clarissant onto the dance floor.

For the first few moments of gliding around the room with the music soaring and one of Tristan's hands on her waist, the other on her hand, and her hand on his shoulder, Clarissant couldn't think, let alone speak. They danced the regulation twelve inches apart, but she kept remembering the day he'd carried her back to the house after she broke her arm. She was twelve and he seventeen and already in love with Rowena, but Clarissant knew she wanted to marry him, a man who could be so tender and gentle that she thought about him carrying her more than she recollected how much her arm hurt.

"Penny for them," Tristan said.

"What? Oh." Clarissant looked down at her feet in ivory satin slippers moving in coordination with Tristan's in black leather dancing pumps. "I've never waltzed before, except in practice of course."

"You're very good."

"So are you."

She felt him shrug beneath her hand. "I've had a bit of practice. We had an Austrian lady aboard ship for a while who decided we all needed to learn to dance."

"A lady aboard a pirate-hunting merchantman?" As soon as she asked the question to tease him, she recalled the note.

"A lady with her husband."

"Ah." Clarissant looked into Tristan's face, close enough to note fine lines around his eyes, as though he'd spent much time peering into the distance.

Pining for England and Rowena?

She barely stopped herself from stepping on his foot, and made herself concentrate rather than mourn what she never had or daydream about what she wanted—love with him. "Tristan, you've been warned to leave England."

He stepped on her foot.

"Ouch." She exclaimed loudly enough for the dancers around them to hear.

Tristan scowled at her. "That was your fault. You should have warned me before saying something like that. Whatever you're talking about."

"I didn't know how."

"Start from the beginning. What sort of note?"

"A warning. A note I received from a street urchin. Well, not an—"

"Stubble it, Clarissant, or tell me the whole from the back."

He looked more annoyed than concerned. So, while they matched their steps again, she began telling him of the incident with the reticule and child and the message. The telling took longer than the music, so they found chairs along the wall far enough away from others to provide privacy and close enough for propriety, though they received several speculative glances.

"So this child has no notion of who the gentleman is," Tristan concluded.

"No, she doesn't." Clarissant drew the note from her reticule. "But I do."

Tristan snatched it out of her hand. "You recognize the handwriting? I don't."

"No, not the handwriting—the scent."

"The what?" Tristan held the paper to his nose. "All I smell is jasmine like you wear."

He'd noticed! Oh, her foolish heart.

She made herself be calm. "No, not jasmine—mildew."

Tristan's hand closed around the note. "Deville." His jaw flexed, jutted. "Why that—" He snapped his teeth together. "To use a child . . . and you . . . he must be guilty and wants to get rid of me before I report him."

"But now he's convinced you, you are sure to go to Bow Street."

"I have no proof it was he. Do you think Bow Street will accept your evidence of the note and Deville smelling alike?"

"No, I suppose not." Clarissant worried her reticule between her hands. "And even if we brought Susan to identify him, no one would believe the word of a street urchin over a baronet."

"Which he knows very well." Tristan looked grim. "She's safe, is she not?"

"Yes, I sent her down to Monmouth." Clarissant smiled at the memory of the child's delight in the notion of fields to run in and lots of milk and cheese and regular baths. "I was afraid . . . for her. And you." She couldn't stop herself from touching his arm.

He patted her hand. "I'm perfectly safe, never you fear. He wouldn't dare harm me."

"He might." Clarissant thought Deville likely to, as he seemed unbalanced. "At least return to Bristol."

He would miss the birthday party that way.

Tristan shook his head. "I want to stay in London. I took an extra two days away to visit my brother, and he asked me to stay and ensure that Gwen marries properly. He should come himself, but with the new baby, he doesn't want to leave his wife." He glanced toward the dancers, then down at the toes of his shoes. "I abandoned Rowena when she needed me. My brother made me realize that I can't abandon Gwen too. With Percy occupied with his new family and the horses, Gwen doesn't have anyone from her family to watch over her. I owe it to her."

Since she watched over her family with care, Clarissant couldn't argue with Tristan on that score. So she sought a different tack. "Will you be of use to Gwen if Deville harms you?" Boldly, she touched his arm and added, "Or me."

He studied her face for an intense minute that sent her heart racing, then looked away. Following his gaze, she saw Rowena holding court in the opposite corner.

"I'm not running away again," he said.

Clarissant's heart ran straight off a cliff—or so it felt, it plummeted so hard. A powerful temptation rose inside her. If she told him the truth about Rowena's marriage right then, the news might distress him enough to send him at least as far as Bristol and likely further afield. She opened her mouth, the words there on her tongue; *Tristan, Rowena married Seasham three months after you joined the Army, not after we thought you dead. And Tom doesn't support us. She didn't marry him for that reason. I support the family with my—*

But her business was a secret she couldn't even confide in Tristan, especially not at Almack's.

Suddenly, the business and the secrets all felt like a burden she no longer wanted to bear. So was the crowded room and Tristan's continuing feelings for Rowena. Clarissant wanted nothing more than to go home and sleep until the birthday party passed. She couldn't bear to think how much Tristan was going to be hurt, and thought to warn him ahead of time. The news might get him out of England, away from danger. But she couldn't tell him of Rowena's treachery in the middle of Almack's.

She didn't even have another opportunity to talk to

Tristan. One of Gwen's beaux asked her to dance, then Lady Sefton presented a handsome and shy young man to her for the final dance. Tristan, she noticed, stood up in a set with his sister and Rowena in the group. He looked boyish and happy, and she realized he likely hadn't had many carefree moments in the past six years. Let him have that night. Tomorrow would come soon enough.

Chapter Twelve

Tomorrow came too soon. On far from enough sleep, Clarissant found herself plunged into a flurry of activity she hadn't shared since the come-out ball.

For that, Rowena did most of the preparation, and those she hired did the rest. Being forced into the party to honor their son's fifth birthday, Rowena refused to lift few of her long, slender and very white fingers to assist. She floated from the nursery to the drawing room on a drift of pink gauze criticizing and complimenting in the same sentence. Clarissant chose to ignore it all. She worried more over Gunters delivering the right confections and enough ice being on hand to keep the ices from melting.

And she worried about Tristan's reaction to learning about Rowena's defection. He seemed not to care that much any longer, but he had drawn away from her the instant Rowena approached him. Clarissant was certain he looked at her with sadness. Besides, he wouldn't make an open display of a broken heart for a married lady. That would be unseemly. But he had enough on his plate with Sir Henry Deville threatening him in an obscure way, about Gwen marrying well, about buying his own ship, about society learning he had made his money from pirates, something those in the Navy weren't even allowed to do. He didn't need the distraction of more hurt.

She couldn't stop it, though. The guests arrived, a handful of young heirs and heiresses in tow under the guardianship of nursemaids, and shunted straight to the nursery for enough sandwiches and cakes to guarantee stomach aches. Everyone complimented Rowena on the fineness of the decorations—blue and silver for the colors of the viscount—and the quality of the refreshments, and the beauty of the trio performing for the guests' entertainment. One of the footmen was performing magic tricks for the children's entertainment.

Rowena accepted the compliments without a word for Clarissant. Not that Clarissant gave it much mind. She'd expected that. She preferred to sit in a corner near the music, sipping a glass of orgeat syrup, and watching the door for Tristan. She intended to waylay him and warm him ahead of time. But he didn't come. So much time passed that she had begun to hope he wouldn't come.

He arrived just as Seasham suggested that the viscount be brought down for inspection. As Tristan paid his respects to his hostess and host, the nursemaid brought Thomas, Viscount Ripon, into the room.

Clarissant liked her nephew. He was a sweet-natured

boy taking after his father in temperament as much as he favored his mother in looks. Good nursemaids and now a tutor were bringing him up to show respect for peers as well as adults, for he would have great responsibility once he reached his majority. Warned to be on his best behavior, he made his bow to the ladies in the room, and shook hands with the gentlemen, charming everyone and making crossing the room to Tristan impossible.

"So how old are you, lad?" came the inevitable question.

"He's four," Rowena said.

"Begging your pardon, Mama," Ripon said with utmost courtesy, "but today I am five."

Clarissant watched Tristan's face, read the confusion, then the understanding that Rowena had been married for six years, not five. She expected him to, at the least, flash Rowena an accusatory glance, and, at the worst, say something aloud.

He did neither. Slowly, he set down his glass, bowed to Seasham, then walked out of the drawing room without giving Rowena so much as a glance.

Tristan paused once on his way out of the Seasham townhouse. At the foot of the steps, he asked the butler when Lord and Lady Seasham married exactly.

The man looked bewildered. "Why, sir, they married six years ago this June."

"Thank you." Tristan left the house without his hat or topcoat. He didn't wait for his phaeton to be delivered from the mews. He started walking faster, faster, and faster until he realized he wasn't suffering the pain of discovering that Rowena had married in June of 1812, three months after their interrupted elopement, not three months after learning of his alleged death. Though he expected and even sought for the same gut-wrenching pain he'd experienced upon learning of Rowena's marriage in the first place, he discovered a different emotion roiling inside him—anger. Not anger with Rowena, anger with Clarissant for not being honest with him. He could accept subterfuge from others. He expected it in society. But not from Clarissant.

Anger mounting, he spun on his heel and marched back to the townhouse and startled the butler. "Send Miss Behn to me now . . . please."

"Sir, she's with Mister Mc—"

"Where?"

"Sir, I don't think—"

"Never you mind." Tristan brushed past the butler and took the steps two at a time. He knew where to find Clarissant with Ian McLean.

He pushed the library door all the way open. As he suspected, Clarissant stood in the center of the room looking up at McLean, her face intent, her hand on his arm. "Ian, why didn't you come tell me sooner?"

"I did not wish to fash—concern you. You've enough to concern you, what with—Mister Apking."

Clarissant released Ian's arm as though it was on fire. When she faced Tristan, she looked decidedly guilty, as well she might, meeting a man alone while the family was otherwise occupied.

Tristan resisted the urge to grab McLean by his coat

collar and drag him into the street. McLean was big enough to fight him, and Tristan didn't want to make a scene.

But he did want rid of the Scotsman of business. "A moment of your time, Clarissant," he said. "Alone."

"I can't." Clarissant glanced at McLean. "Ian—"

"I'm leaving." McLean headed for the door.

Clarissant looked worried. "But you're returning later."

"If I can." McLean bowed, then ran down the stairs.

Tristan closed the door. "You're awfully friendly with him."

"It's none of your concern."

"It is."

"Why?"

"Because—" Tristan faltered on the answer, yet it sprang before him as obvious as a mountain range.

Somehow, while thinking he nursed a broken heart over Rowena, he had fallen in love with Clarissant. Witty, hoydenish, awkward Clarie had grown into witty, gracious, poised Clarissant, and shown him that his love for Rowena had been little more than a schoolboy's fancy, awe for a beautiful face and flattering attention. What he felt for Clarissant ran deeper, stronger, and just as futilely.

When he'd abandoned Rowena to a marriage of convenience to save the family, how could he offer for Clarissant mere weeks after his return? Even if she accepted him—and she apparently cared for another man—her family might object to him. He was a younger son with a fortune gained by pirates.

And he'd been threatened in an oblique way.

They'd all be better off if he did leave England. Clarissant would ensure Gwen didn't marry unwisely. Clarissant would marry Ian . . .

Tristan yanked open the door. "I'm sorry," he said, for too many things to express—sorry that he'd fallen in love with the wrong sister in the first place, sorry that he'd returned to England at all, sorry that he'd returned to Clarissant. But not sorry that he loved her.

She looked about to speak. Then her face closed up, and he caught the drift of roses and violets, a harbinger of Rowena. Schooling his face, he turned to meet her in the doorway. "Lady Seasham?"

"Lady Seasham?" She let out a trill of forced merriment. "Tristan, we're such old friends, how could you be so formal?"

"Because we weren't as good of friends as I thought."

Behind him Clarissant gasped.

Tears filled Rowena's huge blue eyes. "Oh Tristan, how can you be so cruel? But I knew you'd be overset with the party and finding out I married Seasham so soon after you left. But we were so poor! What else could I do?"

"Nothing." Guilt choked off anymore words he might have spoken.

She'd married a rich man to help her family. He must remember that. It rose up as an impenetrable barrier between him and Clarissant.

Rowena dabbed a scrap of lace to her eyes. "I admit I was lonely too, and we had no prospects and Seasham is so kind . . . he's the best of husbands for me, you must see. But I never stopped loving you until . . . until I thought you were dead. Now . . . my husband . . . must love—oh, Tristan, don't look so cold toward me. I didn't want to break your heart. Seasham is just . . . he has money and a title and . . . you must see what I mean."

With a rustle of silk, Clarissant moved past Tristan to slip her arm around Rowena's waist. "Seasham is perfect for you. He adores you, and you have two lovely sons. Go back to your party and let them all see what a fine wife and mother you are."

"I want to be." Rowena turned and glided back into the parlor, still the most beautiful lady he'd ever seen, perhaps more so than even before for the hint of pride in the angle of her head and straightness of her back.

She had married for money to keep her loved ones from starving, and now determined to make that marriage work. He honored her for that. But he no longer loved her. Clarissant was right. If he had loved Rowena more, he would have come home sooner. It wouldn't have made a difference to her marrying Seasham, but Clarissant might not be looking at him as she was in that moment—with irritation.

"Did you have to upset her?" she demanded.

Tristan glared back at her. "Did you have to let me come without a warning?"

"I told you to go back to sea. I was trying to spare your feelings."

"You could have spared them with the truth."

She flinched, and her chin tightened. "Do you truly want to know the truth?"

"I already know it." He flexed and relaxed his hands, flexed them again, pressing them against his thighs.

"And you're right. I should have gone back to sea. Staying here will only cost me more now that I know that I—"

No, he couldn't tell her that he loved her. She wouldn't marry him no matter how much she cared for him. To her, he was only a friend.

But he couldn't resist taking her hand in both of his. "I wish you could have been truthful with me days ago. Now . . . I'll leave for Bristol as soon as I can."

She squeezed his hand. "Tonight. Tristan, leave tonight. For all our sakes, do what Deville or whoever wants and go."

She looked so distressed, he wanted to tease her out of it as he'd always done. "What, you won't miss me?"

"With all my heart." She didn't speak the words aloud, but she formed them with her lips.

"Clarissant?" Stunned at the possibility her words raised, that she really did care for him as more than a friend, he stepped toward her, wanting to sense and see as well as hear her confirm what he wanted to be true. "Will you miss me enough to come to sea with me?"

For a moment, just a flash like summer lightning in an otherwise clear sky, her eyes lit. Then she retreated behind her veil of lashes and shook her head. "I can't. I have commitments here."

"Commitments? Do they have anything to do with Ian McLean?"

"Yes, and my family and—" She yanked her hand free of his. "Do you think I can simply pick up and run off with the same man who wanted to run off with my sister six years ago? Tristan Apking, you're mad. Arrogant and mad to think I'd be such a gullible fool. I am not a substitute for Rowena. I'm—" She pressed her hand to her mouth, the rest of her face registering horror.

As well it might. How dare he be so bold as to ask that of her? How could he think for a moment that she would leave her family for him?

"Forgive me." He gave her a formal bow. "I can't expect you to believe that I love you this soon after you thought I loved Rowena."

She screwed up her face as though concentrating to understand what he'd just told her. Then she shook her head. "No, I can't."

"In time?" He couldn't resist pressing.

She shook her head. "There is no time, Tristan."

She turned her face away.

"Of course not."

"Thank you for coming." She dropped him a formal curtsy, then headed upstairs.

He started to call after her, recalled the servants in the hall below, and beckoned to a footman. "Is Miss Apking in the house?"

He hadn't seen her in the drawing room.

"Yes, sir, she's in the nursery."

Gwen liked children?

"Shall I fetch her for you, sir?"

"Please. I'll wait in the library." Tristan headed across the hall to the quiet, dim room.

A few moments later, light footfalls sounded on the steps in a lull of music from the large drawing room, and Gwen sailed into the library. "You look like a thundercloud. What's amiss?"

Tristan had never considered seeking advice from Gwen. She was so young, but she was Clarissant's friend, and she knew the Behns well. She might know something that would help him decide what to do now.

He affected a nonchalant pose with his shoulders propped against the mantel. "I just learned that Rowena will be celebrating her sixth anniversary next month, not next year. She didn't wait for me long, did she?"

Gwen's lower lip quivered. "Oh, Tris, I'm so sorry you had to find out. I wondered why Seasham made such a fuss about having a party for Ripon. No one has parties for a fifth birthday. But he wanted you to know to make sure you would know—"

"I do now, no thanks to my sister and dear friend Clarissant." Anger renewed inside Tristan. "Why were neither of you honest with me?"

"We didn't want you to be hurt anymore."

"Clarissant's idea?"

Gwen nodded.

Anger evaporated in the wake of tenderness. "Does she think she has to protect everyone's feelings?"

Gwen clapped her hands. "Oh, I knew it. You are in love with her and not Rowena, aren't you?"

Face warming from more than the fire, Tristan nodded. "But how can I even consider courting her, when her sister gave me up to save the family?"

And that little matter of a threat against me?

Gwen's expulsion of laughter made him realize the arrogance of what he'd said, and he laughed too.

"Or so I believed."

"Well, it must be true because they were terribly

poor, and they're doing quite nicely now. But Seasham would have to be quite, quite rich, and I'm not certain of that now that we're in town."

For a moment, Tristan seized on the idea that Rowena had not married Seasham to save her family from poverty, but he shook it off. "He must be wealthier than it appears. How else could they have turned their fortunes around?"

"You did."

"Yes, well, I went into business."

Gwen pouted. "I wish all men would have your good fortune. The nicest ones . . ." She shrugged. "Whatever the truth, Tris, I do think Rowena genuinely cares for Seasham."

"I hope she does." An examination of his heart told him he spoke nothing but the truth. What love he'd had for Rowena had evaporated like water droplets in the sunshine.

Could it have been very strong if it could die so quickly?

"If you love Clarie, why do you look so sad?"

"Two reasons." Tristan looked at his hands, rough and callused from hauling lines and calking seams and firing cannon. "First of all, do you think Clarissant would marry me when her sister wanted to and could not?"

"No, she wouldn't no matter how much she loved you."

"Which brings me to the second reason. Does she love me?"

Gwen walked to the window and held back the drapes to reveal the garden, vibrant beneath spring sunshine. "She cares a great deal about you. But I'm afraid she's in love with Ian McLean."

Tristan's gut clenched. "I feared that too. I've seen them together so often."

The jealousy he'd felt whenever he did see them together should have warned him of how much he cared for Clarissant.

"She rides out with him every day," Gwen continued in a flat little voice. "And the other day she came home with this bottle of ink that smells like lilacs. She tried to tell me she bought it, but I've never seen it in any of the shops. I think Ian gave it to her. Perhaps they make it in Scotland. It's an acceptable gi–gift from–ma—" Her voice broke.

Tristan crossed the room in a few long strides and slipped his arm around her shaking shoulders. "Gwen, why are you crying?"

"Ian. I thought he li–liked me some." She swiped a wrist across her eyes, soiling her glove with tears. "He—that was me with him in the garden the night of the ball. We knew one another, you know. He often came to Monmouth, and we'd talk there. I thought he cared, but here in London . . . and he won't do. He's a younger son with no prospects, and when I talked to him ye–yesterday and asked why he ignores me now, he said that he and Clarie have a–an"—she heaved a huge, sobbing breath—"understanding."

If McLean was the man Tristan suspected of being a traitor to England, he would not have hesitated to report him to the nearest magistrate at that very moment to get him away from two females he loved best.

"He's not good enough for either of you. I'll—"

"You can't do anything to him, Tris."

Tristan made himself think with a modicum of reason. "No, if Clarissant wants him, I am in no position to keep her from having him."

Gwen nodded, sniffling. Then she, too, gathered herself, straightening her shoulders and raising her round chin. "You won't even fight for her?"

"If there's a chance. . . ."

"We'll make one," Gwen declared.

Chapter Thirteen

Clarissant studied the note Ian had brought her a few minutes before Tristan burst in on them. He found it pinned to the door of the perfumery that morning. Below it laid a bundle of half-burned sticks to emphasize the threat in the note.

Perfume burns well. If you wish to save your business and keep it secret, you will get rid of Tristan Apking by tonight.

This threat was more specific than the last. She could accept that Tristan was capable of taking care of himself, could fight off any attempt Deville made to harm him—if Deville was the man threatening Tristan. She wanted him to go for his sake, would prefer to have him at sea and alive than in England and in danger. But she could do nothing to force him to go.

Now she must. Now her business was in danger. With

173

the perfumery gone, a score of men and women would be out of work. Ian would be out of work, and he had family to support. She would be out of an income, and Monmouth had not yet begun to produce in a profitable manner yet. That would take another bountiful harvest or two plus the income from the perfumery she poured into the estate to restore it. Tenants would go without new roofs, and she needed glass for the succession houses to produce enough strawberries to sell in London, where they would bring the highest prices.

Now that Tristan loved her, she needed to make him leave her.

The note blurred before her eyes, and she crumpled it in her fist. Her only choices were to either expose her perfumery herself, thus removing any reason for Deville to use it to blackmail Tristan into leaving England, or report Deville to the magistrate at Bow Street and expose how Tristan had gained his fortune. Tristan would fare the best from the scandal. His looks and the size of his fortune would smooth things over eventually. Yet it might harm Gwen's chances at a good marriage. Besides, if Tristan was wrong about Deville—if they were both wrong about Deville—as the French pirate and the sender of the notes, they could be the ones before the magistrate for defamation of character. Their families would be ruined.

She couldn't betray Tristan's secret. He'd already been betrayed by Rowena. Clarissant was thankful he hadn't discovered how badly he'd been deluded about Rowena's love for him. He might think he loved Clarissant now, but she didn't believe he could have gotten over Rowena enough to not feel the sting of her selfish act of marriage. He still believed she was an angel.

Clarissant couldn't wholly accept that Tristan loved her. Too little time had past. That he discovered it right after learning of Rowena's treachery warned her away.

So she needed to warn Tristan away. The warning failing, she needed to send him away, make him think she didn't care for him so he would have no reason to remain in England.

Except she'd failed. She'd slipped up with those words her lips had formed of their own volition—come too close to letting him know that she adored him.

He thought she loved Ian. Intentionally, she fostered that belief, laying her hand on Ian's arm the instant she heard Tristan coming. Ian, she hoped, only thought she touched him out of concern for the perfumery and his safety.

Not that Ian knew what the note said. He gathered it was some sort of threat, perhaps a disgruntled employee, though they couldn't think who might fit that category, or someone they had dismissed for not working up to their standards. To preserve Tristan's secret, Clarissant had kept the contents of the message to herself.

"I'll see that someone watches the perfumery even when we're closed," Ian assured her.

He would, yet this man was devious, first getting a child to steal her reticule, then locating the perfumery . . . and knowing how important it was to her.

Still clutching the note in her fist, Clarissant paced the floor until Gwen flung herself into the chamber so fast the door banged against the wall. "Tristan says he's in love with you, so why won't you marry him?"

Clarissant tripped on the perfectly smooth carpet and fetched up against the bedpost. "Gwen, you will be the death of me." She rubbed her shoulder. "Or I of you. Your brother does not love me."

"Ninnyhammer, of course he does. I've thought it for days." Gwen slammed the door and bounced on the edge of the mattress. "Surely you can see it. He hates every minute he sees you with I—Mister Mclean." She stuck out her chin. "And so do I. You can't have him."

"No, I can't have Tristan. He needs to go to sea. Perhaps in a year or two—"

"You can't have Ian. He was my beau first, and I haven't found anyone I like better." Gwen's lower lip quivered. "Though I have tried to."

Clarissant closed her eyes. "Heaven forfend. Gwen, he's not just a second son like your brother. He's a fifth son from an impoverished family."

"He's employed in a respectable manner. I mean, a man of business isn't like being in trade."

Clarissant tightened the corners of her lips to keep them from twitching in rye amusement. "It's not enough to support a wife and family. He lives in rented rooms."

"My dowry will pay for—how do you know where he lives?" Gwen glared at Clarissant through narrowed eyes.

Clarissant sighed. "Gwen, I know because he works for me."

"For your brother."

"For my brother with me as his adviser." She wrinkled her nose. "Or did you think Mama managed the estate?"

Gwen gave out an unladylike snort. "But Seasham is his guardian, is he not?"

"No." Clarissant decided she could be honest about this. "I am."

"You?" Gwen bounced so hard she landed on her feet, arms outflung to balance herself—or launch her across the room. "But you're not old enough."

"I'm over my majority and was when Papa died."

"But . . . so you. . . ." Gwen sank onto the bed again without bouncing. "Clarie, are you saying you can marry whomever you please?"

"Yes."

"And Seasham can't stop it?"

"Not even Mama can." Sadness touched Clarissant's heart at the memory of her dying father telling her of his will. It was the first and last time in her life she realized that he even noticed her. "Papa said I had too much sense to need someone telling me how to behave."

Gwen's face crumpled. "Then you can marry Ian if you like."

"I—" She started to say she would not, then recalled that Tristan didn't want Gwen marrying Ian, and nodded. "I've put it under consideration."

"Well, you won't." Gwen sounded like a petulant child, yet looked like a determined woman.

If I marry Tristan, I could sell Ian the perfumery, and Gwen could marry him.

But if she married Tristan, he would stay in England and in danger.

"You can't marry Ian," Clarissant affirmed.

To herself she added, *Yet*.

First, she had to get rid of Tristan, send him packing off to Bristol, then out of the country. Other than giving him the cut direct, Clarissant didn't know how she would accomplish this task, since he stubbornly insisted on remaining in London. In fact, he was the first person she saw after greeting her host and hostess at a rout that evening. Considering that, by the time the Seasham party arrived—an hour late—the townhouse in Berkeley Square was a frightful squeeze, and it appeared as if Tristan was waiting for her. With Rowena and Seasham, Mama and Gwen surrounding her, greeting Tristan, what could she do but offer him a smile and nod.

Apparently taking these as invitations, he tucked her hand into the crook of his elbow and led her into the first series of rooms to see and be seen. "I think routs are the most ridiculous forms of entertainment London has devised. One doesn't get so much as a glass of weak punch, and likely needs a new pair of shoes after standing so long and getting stepped on."

Considering she had had her toes stepped on no less than three times already by persons backing into her, Clarissant could only agree. "I didn't want to come at all. A friend of Ian's invited me to join him in his box at the theater, but Gwen insisted I come here."

That was a flat-out falsehood. Ian did have a friend with a box at the theater, but he hadn't invited her for that night specifically. She had a vague, "You should join us some time," kind of invitation.

She felt the muscles of Tristan's arm tighten. "You spend too much time with that man."

"Not in the least." They entered the next chamber, greeted some acquaintances, and moved on to the third and most crowded room of all. "I should be seeing less of you."

"Why?"

"You need to leave London—now."

"Not while you're haring around London with a mere—good evening, Lady Jersey."

Sally Jersey, always ready to talk up a blue streak with a handsome gentleman, set off chattering with Tristan. She gave Clarissant a vague nod, as though not quite recognizing her but thinking she should, then applied her fan to the detriment of the nose of anyone of an appropriately slight stature who walked by, and laughed and chattered without a breath.

Clarissant considered slipping away. He would never find her again in the crowded rooms, likely two floors' worth. But if she was with him, nothing would happen to him. With Ian or a guard at the perfumery, it was safe too. Deville would not harm anything under her protection.

As though thinking of him conjured him, Sir Henry Deville slouched into the chamber. How he'd gotten invited to the most popular rout of the season, Clarissant could not imagine. Perhaps he had higher connections than she thought of a man of his obvious poverty. That was not good for Tristan, for even if Tristan reported him, a man of influence and connections could turn the tables, and Tristan could find himself behind bars or standing in the prisoner's dock.

Or walking Birdcage Walk to the gallows.

Clarissant shuddered at the thought, and kept her gaze on Deville.

Tristan kept his attention on Lady Jersey, who seemed to enjoy his attention. She was such a lively thing, rising from the depths of scandal with her elopement to Gretna Green years ago, to become a patroness of Almack's.

She was proof that influence and connections weathered scandals. Tristan didn't have either. Nor did Clarissant. Their family titles were too insignificant.

She'd lost sight of Deville while standing mutely beside Tristan, motionless save for the number of times someone jostled her enough to send her skipping to regain her balance. She was about to take hold of Tristan's arm again for security when she caught a whiff of vetivert overlaying that sour scent of mildew, and turned her head.

Sir Henry stood beside her, his broad smile looking out of place in his narrow, bony face. "Miss Behn, you are in looks this evening."

That was a whopper. Her hair would not curl, so she'd coiled it into braids around her head. Her gown was one she hadn't prevented the designer from making to Mama's specifications, so was pale pink and graced with far too many ruffles, making her feel like a statue created of strawberry ice. But as long as Deville graced the gathering, Tristan was safe. So she would be graciousness itself and let him tell all the fibs he liked.

She dropped him a curtsy. "Why, sir, you are too kind. And how are you faring in London this season?"

Deville sighed. "Not as well as I'd like. Now that the war is over, the gentlemen seem to outnumber the ladies."

Under normal circumstances, she'd have found his confession touching, even humorous. But he wasn't eligible, so she could offer him no sympathy or assistance.

Or he probably wasn't eligible.

How could they know? Tristan took a risk remaining in London, yet Deville might not be his enemy.

Clarissant fretted the lace edges of her fan. How did she keep Sir Henry Deville talking when she had nothing to talk to him about?

"You look concerned, Miss Behn," Deville said.

"Concerned?" Clarissant laughed too loudly. "What do I have to concern me?"

"Certainly not Lady Jersey." Deville's lips tightened. "She isn't interested in Mr. Apking."

"Of course she isn't," Clarissant snapped. "She's married. She simply likes to . . . talk . . . to . . ." Her voice trailed off as she watched a footman wend his way through the crush, his well-schooled face tight, his progress persistent and heading as straight as possible toward her—she knew because he met and held her gaze with a pleading look.

"Excuse me." She nodded to Deville and wended her way through the crush to meet him, since a lady could move forward faster than a servant. "What is it?"

He pressed a note into her hand. "The lad who brought this said 'tis urgent." He spoke in a normal voice that could have been heard by no one in the hubbub of a hundred persons talking at once. "He's waiting for your response in the kitchen." He allowed his face to droop into a scowl.

Probably thought she was arranging an assignation.

Afraid the note conveyed something far worse than a rendezvous, Clarissant opened the note with shaking hands. It wasn't another threat against Tristan. It was worse for being something already occurring.

She seized the footman's wrist. "Take me to the lad now."

They couldn't move fast enough. Every passing second drew her closer to ruin, drew her family back to poverty.

The note was a message from Ian informing her that his guard had been struck down, and the perfumery set ablaze.

Clarissant no longer stood beside him. By the time he managed to extricate himself from Lady Jersey's company—not at all wondering why they called her Silence as a jest—Tristan realized Clarissant had vanished into the crush.

Could he blame her? He'd started to escort her, then as good as abandoned her, all for a lady whose tongue ran on wheels. He couldn't even remember what she chattered about, for he thought of Clarissant the entire time, the possibility that, if Rowena loved her husband, he could possibly take his chances with Clarissant. Surely him marrying Clarissant wouldn't distress Rowena if her marriage had become a love match. Many arranged marriages did.

Thinking of arranged marriages, he wondered where Gwen had gotten herself, and began searching for her along with Clarissant. He needn't worry she was with McLean. He would never be invited to a party such as this.

But finding anyone in the over-crowded, over-heated, over-decorated rooms proved close to impossible. He should be able to see Clarissant with her height, but not Gwen or Rowena. They were small females, and their voices would never carry above the hubbub.

Deciding they would see him and hail him, he entered the last room on the first floor. No one. At least no one he knew. The room teemed with dandies wearing extravagant waistcoats and perfumed pomade.

He started up the steps.

"Tris–tan?" Gwen's voice rose over talk and laughter and exclamations so well that the tumult died down. Heads turned.

Gwen darted through the crowd coming and going in the doorway, all the time beckoning to Tristan.

He descended the stairs and grasped her shoulders, giving her a gentle shake. "Gwen, quiet. What are you about?"

"Clarie!" Close, he noticed that she was breathing hard and tears were streaming down her face. "She's eloped. I followed her as far as the front door, and she's eloped with Ian."

Chapter Fourteen

Ian's phaeton waited for Clarissant outside the town-house. She raced down the steps without her cloak, and leaped aboard without waiting for assistance. "So good of you to come—"

A hand shoved the center of her back, and she sprawled facedown over the seat, the edge driving the air from her lungs. *Just like at the come-out ball.* Also like that night, she smelled mildew, this time overlaid with vetivert.

Deville! Sir Henry Deville was abducting her in Ian's phaeton.

What had he done with Ian?

What would he do with her?

Tristan was safe. *Stay that way, my love.*

Before she could catch her breath enough to call out for help, Deville whipped up the horses and sent the vehicle shooting forward. The momentum shoved Claris-sant backward, driving her stays into her lungs and belly until she thought she'd be sick right there down the back of the seat. She tried levering herself up, but needed to hang on to prevent herself from flying over the side. That would free her from Deville—likely as a corpse with a broken neck.

The phaeton spun around a corner, sending her feet swinging into space. She heard a shout, a guffaw, a chorus of cheers.

Her legs were showing!

She gasped, heaved with her arms, and hauled herself onto the seat in the proper direction. Her hair hung over her face. She left it that way so no one recognized her. "Deville . . . let . . . me . . . down . . . now."

"Can't." He raced the phaeton around a corner which sent Clarissant sliding into him.

She gagged on his smell. Moldy wool.

Clinging for her life, she slid as far away from him as possible. She could breathe better now. Perhaps she could scream. She could certainly talk. "Why can't you stop."

"Fool woman, you'll get down."

"Whatever do you want with me?"

"I don't want you." He tooled the vehicle down a narrow alleyway which smelled worse than rotten wool overlaid with nose-stinging smoke in the distance. "I want Apking. Why else would I pretend to pay court to a gawk like you?"

Clarissant wanted to hit him. She didn't think she'd ever hit anyone in her life, but she wanted to bash Deville so hard he fell out of the phaeton. How dare he call her that. Her size was something he would have to contend with.

Once the carriage stopped.

"And if you've harmed Ian," she said through her teeth, "you'll pay twice as hard."

"He's not dead." Deville sounded as offhand as a man could be while sailing down a dark alleyway. "Yet."

She took a deep breath to make certain she still could. "He'd better not be. Ever."

Deville swung the vehicle down an adjoining alleyway so fast she knew he had to have practiced this flight.

Practiced. Planned since he'd first seen Tristan at her come-out ball and known his rig was up?

"Some rig, that—treason."

Anger mounting now that she could breathe, Clarissant gripped the edges of the seat as though they were Deville's scrawny neck, and tried to plan. She didn't have a chance to practice. She must get this right the first time.

"What do Ian and I have to do with Tristan?" she demanded, trying to sound sulky, certain she sounded as furious as she felt.

That was better than fear—fear for Tristan, fear for Ian, fear for herself.

"McLean was in the way." Deville laughed again. "And you are bait."

Clarissant laughed in imitations of one of Rowena's high trills. "Bait? I? That's rich, Sir Henry. Tristan's still in love with my sister."

Deville wheeled the phaeton around a corner onto a winding lane which looked vaguely familiar even in the near darkness. "By the way he reacted to me sending you flowers, I'd say he'll bite."

"He'd have gone away if you'd waited." Wiping her streaming eyes, Clarissant looked about for the means of escape.

The lane forced him to slow, but not enough for her to jump. In the narrow lane, she risked mashing her head on a wall or falling down areaway steps. No one was about at night except slinking figures in the shadows, persons she wouldn't trust to help.

And the smoke was growing thicker. In the distance, she heard the clang of a fire bell, and her heart dropped into her stomach.

No, surely not . . .

She tamped down her apprehensions and made herself keep questioning him. "How will you lure Tristan here?"

Deville snorted. "Simple. I told his sister."

"You're bringing Gwen into—ah!"

The phaeton sped around a curve onto a wider thoroughfare, and Clarissant cried out.

The note about the perfumery burning hadn't been a lie.

"How do you know?" Tristan demanded even as he launched himself out the front door and down the steps, Gwen on his heels. "Which way?"

Gwen pointed to the left. "It was Ian's phaeton. I know it. I've seen her driving with him so many times."

"So have I." Tristan clenched his fists to rein in his anger.

She couldn't elope with McLean. He wouldn't let her.

He sprinted to the driver of a carriage waiting for guests. "Did you see a black and white phaeton drive off a few minutes ago?"

"Aye, that I did." The man screwed up his bearded face. "'Twere a girl inside sittin' on t'seat wrong way around."

"What?" Something like cold fingers brushed down Tristan's spine, and Gwen clutched his arm as though she, too, sensed something wrong with the observation. "What do you mean?"

The coachman scratched his head beneath his top hat. "Weel now, she didn't have her . . . er . . . begging your pardon, milady, but her nether parts weren't on t'seat. She were facing backward like she were sick or sommit."

Tristan took only a moment to make a decision. "I need your carriage."

"Sir?"

"Now."

"But, Tris, how do we know—"

Tristan waved Gwen to silence. "Man, I don't have time to argue with you. I need your carriage—now." Without waiting for a by-your-leave, he sprang onto the box, grasped the startled coachman under his brawny arms, and lifted him to the ground.

"Say now, even if you is a toff, you can't—"

Tristan gathered up the reins. "Gwen, fetch the Watch, or Bow Street, and inform Seasham."

"I want to come . . ." Gwen's and the coachman's cries of protest rang out behind Tristan as he snapped the reins over the backs of the horses and sent them lurching forward. Not until he left the square and headed down a main thoroughfare did he realize he had no notion which way to drive in pursuit, only that he must pursue, find Clarissant and whoever drove that phaeton.

If it was Ian, the man would regret knowing Clarissant. If it was anyone else . . .

Tristan set fears aside and drew up next to a link boy. "Did you see a black and white phaeton go past with a lady inside?"

The boy held out his hand. After Tristan dropped a penny into it, he nodded and pointed.

Tristan sent the horses in that direction, past dark shops and open taverns, skulking beggars and laughing, rich youths. Again and again he asked his question, taking false turns, going back, seeking another source. The coins in his pockets dwindled, died. Too much time passed. If he was right, that Clarissant would never elope sitting backwards on the seat, she was in trouble, in danger, and he feared he knew why. He had to find her before anything happened to her, or he could never forgive himself for staying in England after being warned to leave. Or for caring more about his reputation than his hide and not reporting Deville to the authorities.

He had no reputation once the coachman told his tale. He did care as long as he reached Clarissant in time.

But how could he when the carriage proved too wide for the alleyway down which another link boy said his quarry had raced?

Tristan stood in the opening, peering into the darkness. He could walk in the dimness, but not run, and he needed to run.

"Give me your light," he told the boy.

The youth shook his head. "I needs it to earn me keep."

"Then I'll pay you . . ." His pockets were empty save for his watch, heavy gold bought to impress Rowena.

He drew it out. "This enough?"

The boy's eyes widened. "I'll be arrested for stealin', I will."

"Bring it to my lodgings in the morning, and I'll pay you coin." He gave the lad his direction, then grabbed the boy's smoking torch and ran down the alley.

Burning pitch from the light stung his nostrils, blotting out stench from the alley. But his leather shoes slipped in it. Once he went down, tearing his breeches on the rough cobbles. He sprang up again, limping with the bruised and bleeding knee, and kept going, around a corner, down an even darker and more noisome alley to a winding lane empty, dark and quiet save for the distant clang of a fire bell and shadows that could have come from his torch or persons slinking into doorways.

Which way? Could he ask one of these street people? He still wore his cravat pin, another expensive bauble meant to impress Rowena. Happily he would give it away.

But someone here might slit his throat hoping for more. They'd slit his throat for his silk handkerchief.

And he had no weapon.

Dead, he was of no use to Clarissant, if she needed him. Alive and wasting time on wandering aimlessly through London's twisting lanes, he was as good as useless to her too.

He took the risk, removing the sapphire from his cravat and holding it to the light. "For anyone who can give me information."

No one spoke. No one moved. He might have been alone on the street.

He set the sapphire on the pavement and backed

against the corner formed by a flight of stone steps and a wall, protecting his back and sides from assault.

For too many heartbeats, long enough for his held breath to burn in his lungs, he waited for someone to come forward.

Then, as he exhaled on a sigh of frustration and fear, a diminutive creature leaped from the darkness and snatched up the pin. "Thattaway." A pale hand pointed toward the lights of a busier street a quarter-mile away.

Tristan stared. Why would Deville take Clarissant in that direction. Surely he wouldn't want her to be around people who could help her.

For the first time since learning that Clarissant hadn't been sitting on the phaeton seat, Tristan entertained the notion that she had, after all, eloped with Ian McLean.

"You burned my perfumery!" Clarissant shouted at him. "How could you do this to me?" She launched herself at Sir Henry. He looked frail. Surely she could throw him out of the phaeton.

He knocked her over the head with the butt of a pistol. "I had to lure McLean out so I could steal his phaeton. A note saying the perfumery is on fire seemed as good as any."

Slumped on the floor, sick and dizzy, Clarissant ground her teeth against pain and fury driving her to more rash actions. Think. She had to think.

"Don't attempt that again," Deville said.

"I will." She willed herself not to cry at the pain in her head. "You won't harm Tristan, not after . . . my factory."

She failed at not crying. For Tristan, she could be strong to protect him. For her perfumery, her one true accomplishment, the pain ran clear to her soul.

Did she love her business more than Tristan?

The notion jarred her. Surely she was wrong. Wrong. Wrong.

Then why wouldn't I trust him with the truth about Rowena? To protect the business?

She wouldn't need to tell him about the business now. The perfumery was gone. Well, she would just have to stop the man. He wouldn't harm Tristan as long as she drew breath.

But she had to think not mourn. Perfumeries could be rebuilt. Lives could not be restored.

She looked up through the tangle of her hair and realized Deville had driven past the fire—and it wasn't at her perfumery at all. The fire blazed in an empty warehouse next door, the smoke and crowd around it leading her to believe her building burned.

Angry with herself for believing the worst, Clarissant made herself consider what Deville had said. Lure Ian out. Was Ian inside? Imprisoned? Unconscious? Not dead. Never dead. Whatever state he was in, she would join him soon.

And Tristan?

She could only hope Deville's plan failed, that Gwen couldn't find Tristan. That Tristan wouldn't care enough to follow her.

Why should he? He believed she cared nothing more for him than friendship—a lie, like Rowena's marriage to save the family from ruin, to protect Tristan, and encourage him to leave England. He hadn't, but he might not follow if he believed she'd run off with Ian.

Hope flared, then died. Tristan wouldn't believe she'd eloped. To follow her, he would have to ask if anyone had seen her. Someone would note the odd way she'd been knocked across the seat. Others might think she was foxed. Tristan would know otherwise.

What could she do?

Nothing until she knew Sir Henry's plans.

She would bide her time until he revealed them to her—which he did in moments.

Drawing up the horses, he prodded her with the business end of the pistol. "Get down and do nothing ridiculous. Whether you're alive or not, Apking will come."

Clarissant made a hasty descent, looking around for some form of escape, some weapon. "You seem awfully sure of yourself."

Deville merely stepped down from the phaeton and looped the reins around the railing to the front steps with one hand while holding the pistol on her with the other. The phaeton shone in full light of fire and flambeaux.

One flambeaux burned above the factory door, and Deville reached up to pluck it from its bracket. "Inside."

"The door—"

"Is no longer locked."

Clarissant didn't move. If she went inside, she would have less chance of escape.

Deville shoved the pistol into her spine. "Inside."

Clarissant went slowly. A foot from the front door, her nose began to twitch with odors the fire masked until then. Inside, someone had spilled quantities of perfume oils. Oils. Distilled fragrances. Tinder for a fire.

Her eyes burned, and she began to cough. "We won't be able to breathe."

"You won't have to."

For the first time, Clarissant admitted to herself that Deville intended to kill her too. And Ian? Most definitely Tristan.

She would do whatever she must to stop him.

She seized the doorhandle and pushed the portal in. The smell struck her like a wave, and she buried her face in the crook of her elbow for better breathing. "Don't bring that torch in here. It'll go up like a firework."

"Only a few things in the back corner broke when McLean and I . . . argued." Deville pushed her forward. "Go to the office."

She went, trying to locate a weapon still. Nothing. The bottles were too fragile. Even breaking them would shatter them into fragments too small to use as weapons. Work tables were too heavy. But in the office perhaps . . .

She strode to the office doorway and stopped with a gasp. Ian sat tied to the chair behind the desk, a gag across his mouth. But his eyes were clear and bright with fury, then fear.

"At least you're alive," she said.

He made an inarticulate noise that sounded like a growl.

"I'll get us out," she mouthed.

He blinked. A yes or a no?

No matter. She would do what she could. What she must.

"Go kneel beside him," Deville commanded.

Clarissant twisted her head around to stare at him. "Do what?"

"Go kneel beside him." Deville gestured with the gun. "Take off his gag and untie him, but don't move or make a sound or I shoot one of you. I do believe Mr. Apking has arrived."

Clarissant opened her mouth to deny the claim as being impossible, but at that moment she heard Tristan calling her name.

Chapter Fifteen

At the sight of Clarissant kneeling beside McLean's chair, Tristan halted in the office doorway of what smelled like a perfumery. She had her hand on McLean's shoulder and was whispering in his ear. The scene sickened Tristan.

"I thought you were in danger." He swallowed against an odd tightness in his throat. "But you truly are eloping."

Clarissant shot him a look of annoyance. "Yes, we are, now go away. It's none of your concern."

"It's completely my concern. I love you."

"And I loved her first," McLean said.

Tristan glared at him. "While you were dallying with my sister in the garden?"

"I never dallied—"

"He's been my friend," Clarissant said, "while you were off hunting pirates."

Tristan jumped at her shouting the last word. What in the—

Deville stepped out from behind the door and held a pistol to Clarissant's head. "Foolish of you, Miss Behn. Now I'll have to shoot you."

Clarissant rolled her eyes. "You were going to do that anyhow." Her face was white in the flickering light of the torches Tristan and Deville held, and Tristan wanted to smash the pistol into Deville's teeth for frightening her.

McLean's face darkened except for a white line around his mouth, and, for the first time, Tristan truly believed he loved Clarissant.

"If you help me get her out of this, you can have her," Tristan said.

Deville laughed. "You won't do that, Apking. You're going to shoot both of them, then yourself—or so it will appear."

Tristan made himself laugh too. "Coming it a bit too strong, Deville. No one will believe that. They think I'm in love with her sister."

"Not even Lady Seasham believes that," Deville scoffed. "Now put that torch down and go stand by McLean."

"You only have one shot," Tristan said in as nonchalant a tone as he could muster. "You shoot her, it'll be a fair fight."

"I have more than one pistol." Deville cocked his pistol, making Clarissant flinch. "Put the torch down."

"Be c–careful." He heard her teeth chatter from across the intervening six feet of space. "The perfume oils will go up like gunpowder." Her gaze flickered from one torch to the other to a row of crystal bottles on the desk. "Please don't burn this place down."

Deville snorted. "As though you'll still need it."

"Please *don't* burn this place down," Clarissant repeated. "Please *don't. Don't.*" She gave him a pleading look, and he understood.

"Get behind the desk," Deville commanded.

Stepping forward as though intending to obey, Tristan grabbed a handful of perfume bottles in one hand, noting that they were empty, and flung them with one hand while tossing the torch into the shop with the other hand. With the ring of crystal shattering, the bottles struck Deville's arm, bounced, and struck the floor. Clarissant screamed, dropped, and grabbed Deville's ankles. Deville whipped out another pistol, and McLean launched himself at him from one side while Tristan tackled him from the other. They brought him down with a floor-rattling thud.

With a quiet *woomph,* the outer room caught fire.

Atop the tangle of arms and legs, Tristan rose first, lifting Clarissant with him. "Can you manage him alone, McLean?"

"Aye, sir." McLean brought the butt of a pistol down on Deville's skull with a sickening *thunk.*

Tristan swung Clarissant into his arms despite her protest of being too heavy. "You weigh nothing." He charged through oily black smoke that brought instant tears to his eyes with the reek of too much scent—so much he tasted it and coughed.

Outside the air smelled fresh in comparison, in spite of the embers of the dying fire down the road. Tristan breathed deeply, and raced across the street away from the quickening blaze behind him. McLean joined him, and they set their burdens on the pavement.

"He's out cold," McLean said, nudging Deville with the toe of his boot. "But perhaps I could be having your sash to tie him, Miss Clarissant?"

Without looking at him, she nodded and untied the ribbon. She was gazing at the building, tears streaming down her face.

Tristan encircled her shoulders with one arm. "Did he hurt you?"

She shook her head. "No."

"Are you certain?"

"Yes."

He brushed his fingertips down her cheek. "Then why are you crying? You were so clever to think of distracting him with the fire, we got away. And now any magistrate will believe my report against Deville."

"They don't have to, to see him transported at the least." Clarissant sounded too quiet for someone who had just helped catch a traitor and potential murderer.

He gave her a gentle shake. "Then what's wrong?"

They were drawing a crowd. Those bored with the futile efforts to save the other building, turned their attention to the perfumery and the people who'd raced out of it.

Clarissant took a shuddering breath and faced Tristan. "That factory was mine."

Tristan stared at her. "That factory was what?"

She inclined her head, covering her face with her hair. "The perfumery was mine. It has been for three years. It's how I support the family—with trade."

Beside them, Deville was groaning and trying to sit up. McLean kept the pistol pointed at him while answering the many questions shouted at them.

Tristan ignored the hubbub and onlookers and grasped Clarissant's shoulders. "Explain yourself. Did you say you support the family?"

She looked right into his eyes. "Yes. *I* support the family."

"But   Seasham . . . Rowena's   marriage . . ."   He couldn't think. The clouds of overly perfumed smoke were effecting his thinking. "Seasham supports your family. It's why Rowena married him."

"No, Tristan, it's not." Clarissant shook her head. "He helped me get started, but Seasham never supported us."

Anger rose with understanding. "You're telling me that Rowena didn't marry to save you all from poverty?"

Clarissant nodded. "That's what I'm telling you. She married to save herself from poverty."

Tristan dropped his hands from her shoulders and pressed his fists against his thighs. He turned away from her, one fact looming large and crushing in his mind, in his heart.

Clarissant had allowed him to believe the lie that kept them apart.

A constable pushed through the crowd, his shouted orders indistinct over the roaring in Clarissant's ears. She thought he barked questions and insisted everyone go away except the parties involved. That meant her, but she didn't want to have anything to do with Sir Henry Deville. She wanted to weep alone.

Tears already streamed down her cheeks, though she didn't know if they were for the loss of her shop, for the several bruises starting to ache around her body, or for the sight of Tristan's face as the truth dawned on him. Perhaps she could rebuild her shop if she could find someone willing to loan her the money. With a gun to her head, she'd seen no other way to save the three of them but to start a fire. The bruises would heal. And Tristan?

He'd received another blow, possibly one as great as learning that Rowena was married. He wanted nothing to do with Clarissant, the messenger that tore down the last shred of his dreams about Rowena.

Served him right for falling for a pretty face.

Sickened that she loved a man whose affections ran only skin deep, she turned toward Deville. May as well get the questions finished with.

The image that greeted her glance took her breath away more than the cloying smoke from the fire. Deville lay on the pavement, head and one arm bleeding. Ian was cutting away the sleeve of Deville's coat to make binding the arm wound easier, and Clarissant caught sight of an odd garment beneath his shirt.

She didn't know anything about what gentlemen wore beneath their shirts, but she guessed it wasn't a rough wool shirt that had to chafe his skin.

"It's like a hair shirt," Ian said. "And smells like 'tis damp."

"Mildew," Clarissant said, too weary to have any expression in her tone. "He always smelled like mildew. He must have worn this a long time."

"Since the pirate ship days," Tristan murmured. "A rough shirt to chafe his skin like people a few hundred years ago to punish themselves."

"I ken naught about pirates," Ian said, "but if he's done wrong, he's punishing himself for it."

"He has a conscience." Clarissant knelt beside Sir Henry and tore off the flounce on her petticoat to bind up his head. "We can't let him hang."

"Do you have to protect everyone?" Tristan didn't sound happy with her. "He nearly killed you."

"And he burned down my livelihood," Ian added.

Tristan shot him a withering glare. "So you were in on this too?"

Ian flashed Clarissant a questioning look.

She sighed. "Yes, he was. He's really my perfumery manager, not the man of business for the estate. Mossy and I take care of that for Dunstan, but he's so good with numbers and crops and things, he's . . . about . . ." She was talking too much, and nearly jumped up and hugged the constable for clearing away the crowd and approaching them.

"You've some explaining to do," he said. "Come to Bow Street, and bring your friend with you."

"You'll be needing your horses," a gangly youth announced. "I moved 'em outta the fire, 'cause they was getting wild." He held out his hand. "Want me to tell you where they are?"

Tristan grimaced. "We should have thought of them. And here I am with my ready spent."

Ian looked down. "I came away too quick to bring any coin."

To her amazement, Clarissant realized that her reticule still hung from her arm. Inside, she carried a handful of sixpences and shillings, and offered a few to the youth. He took them, then pointed down an alley. "There's a yard back there. Shall I fetch 'em?" He held out his hand again.

Clarissant started to put another coin in it.

Tristan snatched the coin away and gave the youth the gold buckles from his shoes. "They're worth more than a shilling."

The youth nodded and ran to the alley.

"How will you walk now?" Clarissant asked.

"Taller for knowing that you didn't completely get me out of this fix." With that, he stood and shuffled after the youth.

She didn't talk to him again that night. First, she had to tell her story to a sleepy magistrate. Sir Henry woke in time to tell his story. He'd been captured by the pirates while sailing to India to make his fortune, and fought beside them to keep himself out of the hold or being killed.

"I suppose," he concluded wearily, "a true Englishman would have died rather than fight his countryman, but I'm a coward."

No one disagreed with him.

Then, after an uncomfortable silence, Tristan leaned toward him. "Why did you follow Miss Behn around?"

"I wanted to know your movements from her." Sir Henry rubbed his bloodshot eyes. "I wanted to know how important she was to you. Weapons to use against you."

"Weapons." Tristan made a noise rather like a growl. "And why did you want to kill me? I hadn't yet reported you to the magistrate, and I had no intention of reporting you. I wasn't certain you were the same man I fought that day. You were safe."

Sir Henry gave him a contemptuous glare. "I knew you wouldn't risk maligning my character and letting others know how you gained your fortune. But the fact that you have that fortune is enough to make you worth destroying."

Clarissant thought her face must look as blank as those of the others.

Sir Henry sighed. "He stole it from me. I gave up my honor for that fortune, and he and his lot stole it in one day."

After that pronouncement, the magistrate locked Sir Henry in a cell there instead of hauling him off to Newgate Prison, and Ian drove Clarissant home. Tristan walked off somewhere, shoes flapping without their buckles.

At the Seasham townhouse, Clarissant had more than a few ruffled feathers to soothe. Gwen shot her a withering glare, then stalked off muttering something about sleeping in a guest room. Mama looked confused and wandered off to her bedchamber murmuring something about thinking Clarissant would marry someone besides a Scot. Miss Moss scolded over the state of Clarissant's clothes, hair and, when she noticed, person, and ushered her to her bedchamber with orders to go to bed at once and drink the hot posset she would prepare herself. Rowena was annoyed, standing in the middle of the bedchamber rug, railing about Clarissant ruining her chances for a good match.

Clarissant was too fatigued to argue with her sister, but thought to be rid of her. "I never had a chance at a good match, Row. I'm in trade, and my husband would not have liked that, so I wouldn't get as far as having a husband."

"Except for Ian McLean." Rowena stomped her foot. "The least you could have done for me is marry Tristan."

Clarissant whipped on her dressing gown so she could emerge from behind the dressing screen and stare at her sister. "You *want* me to marry Tristan?"

"Well, of course, why wouldn't I?" Rowena looked annoyed. "It would stop him from dangling after me."

Clarissant started to laugh. Admittedly, it held a note of hysteria, and she made herself stop at once. But that was rich, the momentary notion that Rowena intended to be selfless in giving her permission for Clarissant to marry Tristan because she, Rowena, no longer wanted him around.

Clarissant sank onto the bed, too weary to stand. "I'd prefer a husband who is more than fond. He needs to at least respect me."

And Tristan hadn't appeared particularly full of respect for her when he walked away from Bow Street.

"Respect you?" Rowena flung back her head and laughed this time. "Who will respect you once they learn you've been in trade?"

Clarissant stood, towering over her sister. "That trade you scoff at kept us housed and clothed so that your husband didn't feel responsible for supporting us, so that you could have a Grosvenor Square townhouse. Or would you prefer that your family languished in poverty while you ate lobster patties?"

"Oh, you're cruel." Rowena burst into tears and fled the bedchamber.

Clarissant suppressed the urge to go after her. For once in her life, she'd been honest with Rowena, and she had Seasham to comfort her. Already, Clarissant heard him soothing Rowena's ruffled feathers. Rowena had her husband to protect her. Clarissant no longer needed to do so.

She sat on the bed, fatigued to her marrow and wondering how her attempts to take care of everyone led to having all of them angry with her.

Clarissant hefted the flat basket of roses, barely dry of morning dew, onto her shoulder and trudged toward her workshop. A swarm of bees followed her. She tried to ignore them as much as she tried to ignore the rumble of carriage wheels on the drive. No one, unless addlepated, would visit Monmouth this early, especially now that she had been banished there until another scandal took precedent over the one regarding her being in trade. Sales of stock already in shops dropped to a handful a week instead of dozens a day. She canceled her cargo space on a merchantman, and sold her stock of perfumes and inks to Ian. He intended to start the business again, and had found investors willing to back a man in business.

"But I still need your nose," he added. "Will you still create scents for us—for a fee, of course?"

Because she didn't want all those men and women to

be out of work any longer, Clarissant agreed. What else did she have to do?

True, Dunstan wanted her to teach him how to manage the estate on his own, and little Susan had taken a fancy to perfume creating and book learning. She also cleaned everything she could find, making the maids fear for their positions if every speck of dust and grime didn't disappear from the house in an instant. Susan even tried cleaning the stable, but the groom picked her up by the collar of her dress and carried her out with orders never to return until she wanted to ride.

"We need to make scented soap," Susan informed Clarissant. "Not just for bathing, for scrubbing too. The lye fair burns me nose. What do you think of lemon?"

Remembering the maid's suggestions for laundry soap, and Susan's enthusiasm for doing anything useful and clean, Clarissant smiled on her way around the outbuildings to her workshop. She would take Susan on as an apprentice too.

Despite the early hour, she heard Gwen's laughter, and started to turn away. She was too weary from picking roses—she was on her tenth trip back to the workshop—to face Gwen and whomever she spoke with. It wasn't her. Until recently, Gwen had barely spoken to her since the night of the fire.

After Rowena fled Clarissant's room, Gwen stormed from the guest chamber across the hall and gave Clarissant the worst tongue-lashing of the evening. The more Clarissant tried to explain she intended to protect Gwen from marrying into a potential scandal, the angrier Gwen became.

"You weren't trying to protect me," she accused.

"You were trying to protect your business. If Ian truly were your man of business for the estate, you'd have given your blessing on our union."

Clarissant opened her mouth to deny the claim, but shut it again, knowing Gwen was absolutely right.

"I'm sorry," was all she could say.

She was sorry, for now Ian seemed to have no interest in Gwen, even avoided her whenever he came to Monmouth. "I need to get the business going again before I can think of a wife," was his explanation.

As for Gwen, she didn't lack for suitors. When Rowena decided to retire to the North with Seasham and the children, Gwen retired to Monmouth where she was still close enough to London for her string of admirers to call on her. The local innkeeper had grown so fond of the extra custom she brought him through all the young men staying there that he kept sending her his wife's famous pies and scones in appreciation.

Clarissant presumed Gwen laughed over another pastry tribute or a beau so eager to see her he arrived before eight of the clock.

Not caring if anyone saw her in her faded gown that barely skimmed the tops of her half-boots, and her hair hanging in a single plait down her back, Clarissant tramped around the corner of the last outbuilding, head down—and walked into Tristan.

The basket flew out of her hands. Roses soared in half a dozen directions, angered bees swooped. Clarissant ducked to avoid roses and bees, slipped on the gravel, and landed on her knees at Tristan's feet. A shout from him warned that he had not evaded an assault.

"I told you to warn her you were coming." Gwen sounded smug.

Nursing one hand in the other, Tristan glared at her with storm-cloud eyes. "At the least you have more sense about that than the beaux you choose. Or have you decided to stop tossing your cap for McLean?"

Gwen flounced her red curls. "I don't need to toss my cap for him. Are you all right, Clarie?"

Her knees burning, Clarissant nodded.

"Tris," Gwen commanded, "help her up."

"I don't know." Tristan gazed down at Clarissant. "I rather like seeing her kneeling before me."

Gwen punched his arm, then held out her hand for Clarissant. "Here, let me help you up."

Clarissant scrambled to her feet on her own. "I'm sorry to interrupt. Let me gather these roses and be—"

"Stubble it," Tristan fairly growled. "You've played the martyr long enough. Besides, I need you to remove this stinger."

Clarissant looked at the roses to see if she could salvage any. "I didn't think you needed my help with—ah!"

Tristan kissed her. "That should keep her quiet for a moment."

Gwen laughed.

Clarissant slumped against the workshop wall.

"I'll be off now," Gwen said. "Sir Charles is coming to—"

"Don't." Clarissant found enough of her voice and senses to panic at the idea of being alone with Tristan, especially after . . .

Well, what was he doing kissing her?

"You surely don't dislike me this much to leave me alone," Clarissant concluded.

Gwen looked puzzled. "I don't dislike you at all."

"When you've scarce spoken to me in weeks?"

Gwen shrugged. "Oh, that."

"She hasn't spoken to me either," Tristan said. "Something about bull-headed men and you being as bad."

"I only wanted the best for everyone," Clarissant said, but hearing it aloud, she wondered if she told the truth.

The way Gwen and Tristan looked at her said they thought the same.

She sighed and bowed her head. "I liked having the power to manage everybody's lives. No one ever seemed to manage anything well, and I thought I could do a better job of it. But I hurt you all along the way."

"Not me," Gwen said. "I was hurt over Ian at first, but not anymore."

Tristan said nothing, and, despite the kiss, Clarissant felt her heart break all over again.

She dropped to her knees and began gathering roses. "I'll just take these—"

"Nowhere." Tristan crouched before her and covered her hands with his. "You're not going anywhere yet."

"But I am," Gwen sang out, then scampered toward the house.

Clarissant dared look at Tristan. "Please, go away. You've wanted nothing to do with me for weeks, now I want nothing to do with you."

Tristan kissed her again. "Now tell me that again."

Clarissant squared her shoulders. "You've wanted nothing to do with me for weeks."

"And."

"Now I–I . . ." She stared down at the roses clutched in her hands. How peculiar. They still looked like they carried morning dew, droplets shining in the sunlight.

"You what, Clarissant?" Tristan's voice was low, gentle.

Clarissant realized she looked on her own tears and crushed the flowers between her hands. "All right, I'll say it, the truth this time. I want everything to do with you. I always have. But you loved Rowena, and now you haven't spoken to me . . ."

She ran out of breath, out of words to express her pain over the past three weeks since she last saw him.

Tristan cupped her chin in his hands and gently tilted her face up to his. "I admit I was angry with you for keeping the truth from me. I thought you considered me so weak I'd crumple if I knew Rowena never truly cared a whit for me. But I'd already worked that out for myself. The Rowena I dreamed about when I was gone doesn't exist." He brushed his thumb across her cheek. "But you do."

"I always have. I was just never good enough as I was. Too tall. Too blunt."

"Too bossy."

She stuck out her tongue at him.

He laughed, then lifted her to her feet. "That's my girl. At least . . ." He stood gazing at her, pleading with his eyes.

His "too bossy" echoing in her head, Clarissant

would not let him off the hook so easily as to say she'd like to be his girl, his lady, his wife—if that was what he wanted. She might hope it for all she was worth and more, but he would have to ask.

"As I've said," she pointed out, "you stayed away for weeks without a word."

"I was hurt and angry." Tristan flexed one hand and winced.

The stinger stayed in the flesh on the back. His jaw hardening, he grasped that with his other hand and yanked.

Clarissant flinched for him. "It'll feel better now that it's removed."

"I hope you're correct in that." Tristan grimaced. "I was wrong to think I could remove you from my life and be all right. I wanted to. I wanted nothing to do with another deceitful, heart-stealing"—his voice softened—"beautiful Behn lady. But life without your wit and sharp tongue and . . ."—he grinned—". . . I love you, Clarissant."

Her heart leaped with joy, but she held it under control. "Then why did you stay away so long?"

"I wanted to make certain for both our sakes. I didn't know . . . after I learned how you didn't trust me to know about the perfumery or Rowena's husband not supporting the family . . ." He rested his cheek against hers. "I've been terribly occupied these past few weeks, but I couldn't stop thinking about how you were the best friend I ever had, and you kept all those secrets to protect me because you loved me like your family."

"But not like my brother." There, she admitted it.

Tristan chuckled. "I'm glad of that. I stopped think-ing of you as another little sister the night of the ball."

"But that one morning in town—"

"I was confused."

"And you were so angry with me the night of the fire."

"Until McLean pointed out that you'd burned down your precious business to save my life."

"My own life—"

"Which was forfeit because of me."

She raised her hand to touch his soft, thick hair. "You came after me, when surely you knew it meant danger."

"When I walked into that shop, I thought you were eloping with McLean."

"You were supposed to." She shuddered, remember-ing. "But Ian's only my good friend."

"He's a very good friend."

She drew back so she could look at his face. "You've decided not to dislike him?"

Tristan shrugged. "He doesn't have a claim on you. Now I just have to stop him from having a claim on my sister, but I'm afraid that's not likely to stop."

Clarissant stared at him. "But Gwen doesn't care about him anymore."

"Ha. That's her game—make us think she doesn't—but they're seeing one another often."

"But—"

Tristan brushed his fingers across her lips. "Don't talk about Gwen and McLean. He's likely to become my brother-in-law yet, and that'll be all right, since he's my business partner."

Clarissant stiffened. "Your what?"

"Well, um, I invested in the perfumery." His eyes expressed panic. "Does it make a difference to you?"

She laid an assuring hand on his arm, forgetting that hand held roses and crushing them against his sleeve. "No, but why?"

His smile was gentle. "So even if you don't want to marry me, I'll still have reason to see you often."

"Oh, Tristan." Her heart completely malleable in her chest, she peeked up at him through her lashes. "But how do you know whether you do or not if you haven't asked me?"

"I had to know if you loved me first." Without warning, Tristan dropped to one knee and clasped her hand in both of his. "Will you marry me, Clarissant?"

Clarissant bowed her head. "I'd say tomorrow, but Rowena will want to plan and—oh!"

On his feet in a flash, Tristan picked her up and twirled her around as though she weighed no more than little Susan. When he set her on her feet again, breathless and laughing, he released her as though he'd been stung again and glowered at the sleeve of his coat. "What did you do?"

"Oh, the roses! I've crushed them."

Tristan wrinkled his nose as though something smelled foul. "My love, my dearest Clarissant, will you do me one favor?"

She tilted her head to one side. "Perhaps."

"Whatever flowers Rowena wants at the wedding, please make certain they're not roses."